Gripped Part 2
Blindsided

Written by Stacy A. Padula
Edited by Michael Mattes

Briley & Baxter Publications | Plymouth, Massachusetts

ISBN: 978-1-7331536-0-7

Book Design: Stacy O'Halloran

Dedicated to Briley & Baxter O'Halloran
@two_cuddly_dachshunds

Preface

To Readers Across America:

Each day, more and more young adults fall prey to substance abuse. As an educator who works mainly with high school students, I was moved to write a book series for teenagers that shares how *it* happens—how good kids become drug addicts, how downward spirals start, how harmless fun can quickly turn into a life-threatening addiction.

The story told in the series is raw and realistic. I did not censor much of the content, for I believe the truth is important and powerful. In our world in which twelve-year-olds overdose in middle school bathrooms, it is time for authors to stop sugarcoating their content to appease schoolboards. I am aware that this book may be banned by public schools because of the harsh realities portrayed between its covers. However, I did not write any part of the *Gripped* book series in hopes of it being taught in English classrooms. The truth is far too controversial for that, even though the events depicted in *Gripped* happen daily across America.

The series portrays the story of Taylor Dunkin who was an acclaimed college athlete, seemingly destined for the NFL but sidelined by injury. His depression leads him to begin abusing his pain medication and eventually become a drug dealer to support his habit. He supplies drugs to high school students from his hometown, which leads to other characters becoming ensnared. The story shows how drug abuse can skew individuals' values and change their perspectives. It follows other characters such as Luke Davids, Cathy Kagelli, Chris Dunkin, and Jason Davids (also featured in my *Montgomery Lake High* book series) whose lives have been affected by Taylor's decisions. It shows the psychological, biological, and environmental reasons behind why people often begin experimenting with drugs and how slippery the slope can be. Most importantly, this book series educates readers on how people can pick up the pieces of their lives and recover from such a horrific epidemic.

I have written five other young adult novels that address teenage social issues. They comprise the *Montgomery Lake High* book series, which is available at Barnes and Noble and Amazon. Over the past eight years, the books have frequently been on the Amazon top 100 best seller list for young adult books that address substance abuse. In the fall of 2017, four of the books were top 10 best sellers within the category. Considering the sharp rise in prescription drug overdoses and opiate abuse, I feel that this book series is needed now more than ever. Please join me in helping to protect the youth from opiate and benzodiazepine abuse by recommending the *Gripped* book series to a teenager you know.

Sincerely,
Stacy A. Padula

Meet the Characters

Taylor

Cathy

Marc

Alyssa

Chris

Lisa

Jason

Luke

Jon

Bryan

Chantal

Character Background
Information

Taylor Dunkin – Taylor was the quarterback for Northeastern University and ranked by ESPN as an NFL Top Prospect until he tore his ACL, MCL, and both menisci during a football game in 2016. He became addicted to painkillers after his second knee surgery and began dealing drugs to support his habit. He and his crime ring are currently being investigated by the Boston Police.

Marc Dunkin – Marc is Taylor's youngest brother and a senior at Montgomery Lake High School. He is committed to attend Boston College in the fall of 2018. In November of 2017, he found out that Taylor was selling drugs to Luke Davids—Marc's best friend—and that Luke was giving drugs to kids from their hometown. Marc has since set off to reverse the damage caused by Luke and Taylor.

Jordan Dunkin – Jordan is the middle Dunkin brother. He is a college sophomore, who plays football for the University of Notre Dame. Marc and Jordan had a falling out during Jordan's senior year of high school over a girl they both liked—Michelle Taylor.

Chris Dunkin – Chris is the younger cousin of Marc, Jordan, and Taylor. He is a freshman at Montgomery Lake High School. His parents travel frequently for their business based in London, so Chris has grown up being very close with his older cousins, who frequently babysit him. Chris began partying at a very young age and experimented with many different drugs in middle school. Today, however, he is completely sober.

Jason Davids – Jason, like Chris, is a freshman at Montgomery Lake High. He is well known for his wit, humor, and charisma. He was in a long-term relationship with Cathy Kagelli until November of 2017. At the beginning of the schoolyear, Jason made many mistakes that he desperately wants to fix. He is determined to win back Cathy's heart.

Cathy Kagelli – Cathy is a freshman at Montgomery Lake High School, known for her beauty and intelligence. She dated Jason Davids until November of 2017 and has been seeing Marc Dunkin since December of 2017. Cathy has struggled with anxiety and depression since she and her identical twin sister, Chantal, had a falling out in 2016.

Chantal Kagelli – Chantal is Cathy's identical twin, also a freshman at Montgomery Lake High School. She is a kind hearted, devout Christian, known for her optimism. For a year and a half, she erroneously believed that Cathy pretended to be her and broke up with her middle-school boyfriend, Jon Anderson. She just found out that the breakup was a huge misunderstanding on Jon's part and that Cathy never backstabbed her.

Prologue
Scenes from Gripped Part 1

Present Day – March 2018

Sitting on the bleachers inside the gym, Jason watched as Chantal reacted to the story he had just shared with her. She took a deep breath. "Wait," she huffed while gaping at him. "Cathy didn't deliberately break up me and Jon?!"

Jason was a bit taken aback by her question. "Of course not," he said in a perplexed manner. "You thought *she* broke you up?"

Chantal's green eyes were glazed with tears. Slowly, she nodded. "She became close with Alyssa after our breakup, and Lisa was so happy to see me with Andy. I heard at church that Jon was claiming he never broke up with me, so I convinced myself that Cathy, Alyssa, and Lisa had somehow plotted the breakup. I knew Cathy was mad at Jon, so it made sense. I assumed she pretended to be me and broke up with him."

Jason widened his eyes. "She would never have done something like that," he stated defensively and lowered his eyebrows. "Her relationship with you meant the world to her. Alyssa had nothing to do with any of it, and Lisa only wanted to see you treated right. Jon was being a jerk, and we wanted to protect you from him."

"I knew Cathy was somehow responsible," Chantal said. "I can't explain how I knew, but I knew. I guess… I guess… I assumed the absolute worst. When Andy was in the hospital last fall, Jon came to visit me. When he mentioned I broke up with him in a voicemail, I completely forgot about the message Cathy left him on the day of our breakup. It never once crossed my mind. I automatically assumed she pretended to be me. I told him that. I told Alyssa that when I became friends with her again. I told a lot of people that," she admitted as her voice cracked.

"Why did you assume the worst?" Jason asked, searching Chantal's eyes. He had always thought of her as someone who saw the best in others.

Tears began seeping from Chantal's eyes. "Because Cathy was acting psychotic at the time," she replied, "to you, to me, to my parents, to everyone."

Jason swallowed the large lump in his throat and took a deep breath before speaking. "I know you're already late for cheerleading practice—"

"I can't go to practice like this," Chantal interrupted him and wiped tears from her eyes.

"Well, if you can hang out a little longer, I can tell you the rest of the story," Jason said compassionately. "It's going to be really hard to hear, especially because your relationship had a lot to do with it, but I think you should know the truth."

Chantal nodded. "Tell me. Don't hold anything back," she said. "Tell me why my sister turned into a narcissist and why she gave up on trying to fix our relationship. Tell me about the drugs—what they are and how they got a grip on her. Tell me everything."

"I will," Jason said, "and you'll finally understand why I am to blame for the shattered person Cathy is today."

Tears had continued streaming down Chantal's face. "I can't believe I assumed such horrible things," she expressed sadly. "It should have dawned on me that I was being judgmental. Love sees no evil, but when I looked at Cathy, all I saw was evil." Chantal took a deep breath. She looked as though the wind had been knocked out of her.

While Luke and Cathy were still outside on his balcony, Taylor picked his iPhone up off the coffee table. Navigating to Instagram, he opened Luke's profile. Months earlier, Marc had blocked Taylor from

5

all of his social media accounts, but thankfully Luke frequently posted pictures with Marc and their friends.

Taylor had recently noticed a girl beside Marc in a lot of pictures, and he assumed Marc was hooking up with her—Marc didn't usually "date" anyone. When Cathy walked through the door, Taylor thought she looked familiar. Only after Luke introduced them did he correlate her with Jason. As they were talking, Taylor began wondering why Luke was hanging out with his little brother's ex-girlfriend and why Cathy seemed so uncomfortable. Then something occurred to him.

Scrolling to a picture from the previous night, Taylor saw Luke in his MLH hockey jersey with his girlfriend Missy, his brother Matt, Marc, and a girl who looked just like Cathy. Knowing Cathy was a twin, Taylor checked to see who was tagged: @ckagelli99. After touching the tag, he was brought to a profile that, indeed, said Cathaleen. As he scrolled through her page, he saw pictures of her and Marc that dated back to Christmas. Knowing how against drugs Marc was, Taylor was surprised he would go out with Cathy. She was pretty, but even Taylor knew she and Jason had experimented with worse drugs than weed or alcohol.

As Taylor closed out of Instagram, flashbacks of the last time he saw Marc infiltrated his mind. He could not believe he had let his youngest brother see him in such a state of weakness. After enduring a week and a half of withdrawal pains and feeling like his skin was crawling for nearly a month, Taylor never wanted to see an opiate again, and he certainly didn't want anyone he knew getting mixed up in them. The amount of guilt he harbored over selling Xanax and Vicodin to Luke was overwhelming. He was fearful that Luke had gotten numerous kids from Montgomery into benzos and painkillers.

After much soul-searching, Taylor realized that his drug problem had begun long before his injury. Since his freshman year in college, he had thought that sporadically dabbling with substances such as coke and molly equated to harmless fun. Because he formed no addictions prior to his injury, he had perceived no danger in partying

6

hard during the offseason. In hindsight, Taylor could see that using drugs warped his values, causing him to prioritize his social life over his football career. Instead of transferring colleges as a sophomore, he had chosen to remain at Northeastern, simply because he was comfortable there—his professors, coaches, and friends adored him. In retrospect, he loathed himself for that decision. Taylor was extremely ashamed of the person he had become and, with newfound clarity, was in awe of the way drugs had not only skewed his perception, but also changed his ambitions.

A moment later, Cathy and Luke came back inside the apartment, interrupting Taylor's thoughts. At the sight of Cathy, he felt incredibly awkward. He did not want Marc or anyone in his family to find out that he was still dealing drugs. Four months prior, Taylor had used his father's money as planned: to pay off his supplier and move away from the negative influences in his life. His supplier, however, had put an enormous amount of pressure on him to sell another batch, saying that would allot him time to find another distributer at the college level. Taylor knew his supplier was well-connected to criminals who would not think twice about taking him out, so he agreed to sell one more stash—free of opiates—out of fear alone. However, after each sale, Taylor felt guiltier and guiltier.

"So, I talked Cathy into taking the Xanax you found," Luke announced before sitting down on the couch.

As Taylor watched Cathy's green eyes drop to the floor, his heart began to pound. "You know what? I think what I found is the stuff my doctor prescribed to help me sleep. You probably don't want this, Cathy," he said and peered at her, hoping she would refuse the drug. He wasn't lying: last month, his doctor prescribed him a low dose of Xanax to mitigate his insomnia.

Cathy let out what sounded like a sigh of relief. "It's probably for the best," she said and sat down beside Luke. She looked up at Taylor and spread her pale lips into a slight smile.

"So, we are thinking of going to lunch somewhere on Broadway. Want to come?" Luke asked.

"I'm good, but thanks," Taylor replied. "I actually have some business to take care of at Northeastern this afternoon."

"Oh, no way, man? That's great. Are you thinking of going back?" Luke inquired.

Taylor shrugged. "I have to straighten out my transcript and see what my options are. I doubt Northeastern will readmit me, but I'm going to talk with my old advisor and find out what's possible. I'm looking into transferring, but I think my grades from last year are going to be problematic."

"I'm sure you'll be able to figure something out," Luke remarked.

"I've got to do whatever it takes to get back on the field. I'm eligible for one more season of D-I ball. That's it."

Luke smiled. "Marc would be so happy to know you're thinking about school again. I would tell him, but he probably shouldn't know we saw each other today."

Taylor laughed awkwardly. "Yeah… I'll tell him soon. He's been waiting way too long for me to get my act together."

Luke cocked his head to the side and widened his hazel eyes. "Are you not selling painkillers anymore?"

Taylor assumed Luke had finally realized he was clean. "No, man. You don't want those things anyway—trust me."

To Taylor's surprise, Luke did not look at all disappointed. In fact, he seemed happy to hear the news. Cathy certainly looked relieved. Perhaps it was a gift that two of Marc's closest companions were there to hear about the positive changes Taylor had been making to his lifestyle.

At Boston College, Marc was going over the current roster with one of his future coaches when a middle-aged man, wearing a blue collared shirt and khakis, walked into the office. Marc assumed he was a professor until he asked for Marc directly.

"I'll let you two talk," the coach said and quickly scurried out of the room, closing the door behind him. Marc was perplexed. He gazed warily at the man, who was taking a seat across from him at the table.

"Hi, Marc," the man said. "I'm Detective Roth of the BPD."

Marc took a deep breath. "Is my brother dead?" he asked in a somber tone.

"No," Detective Roth replied and shook his head.

Marc felt the color return to his face as he let out a heavy sigh of relief.

"You are right to be concerned about him, though," the detective commented. "I need you to get a message to him." He pulled a black cell phone out of his briefcase and handed it to Marc. "Tell him, we know he wants out of the game, and we can make that happen. Have him call the number programmed into that phone when he's ready to discuss his options. Tell him he needs to use great discretion and that he cannot use that phone in public or for any other calls."

"Why are you giving this to me?" Marc asked. "I haven't spoken to Taylor in months."

"He's likely being watched by criminals who can't see him make contact with anyone on the police force," Detective Roth said. "That would put his life in danger, but they won't think anything of you stopping by his apartment."

"He's being watched?" Marc asked and swallowed deeply. "How bad is it?"

"From one Eagle to another," Detective Roth said and raised his eyebrows, "really bad."

Marc's heart began to pound against his muscular chest and his throat went completely dry. "I'll do whatever you need me to do," he pledged in a solemn tone.

"The less involved you have to be, the better," Detective Roth said. "You and your brother Jordan are good kids, and you don't want anything to do with the mess Taylor has entangled himself in. We just need you to open the line of communication for us, and then your role is done. Okay?"

Marc nodded, bewildered that the detective knew about him and his family.

"Taylor will want to talk to us," Detective Roth said. "He's clean and ready."

Marc raised his eyebrows. "He is? How do you know?"

Detective Roth smiled. "The less you know, the better. Can you get that phone to him today?"

Marc nodded. "Yeah, I can call him when I leave here and ask to drop by. If he's home, I'll go right over."

"The sooner, the better," the detective stated. He reached across the table to shake Marc's hand before standing up to leave the room.

"How did you know I was here?" Marc questioned him.

"My boss set up your meeting," Detective Roth replied. "You're important to this school."

Marc stared at the detective thoughtfully. How could his importance to BC's football team have anything to do with Taylor being a drug dealer? He could tell from the detective's somber tone, however, that getting the cell phone to Taylor was imperative.

Chapter 1

Present Day – March of 2018

Taylor Dunkin sighed after shutting his front door behind Luke Davids and Cathy Kagelli. When Luke asked to stop by earlier that afternoon, Taylor feared he would want to buy drugs. After sending Luke off with molly and cocaine, Taylor hoped Marc would not find out about their rendezvous. He knew Luke would also want to keep it a secret, but he feared Cathy would divulge the information. More than anything, Taylor wanted to make things right with his brother. The dissension between Marc and himself bothered Taylor more than any other consequence of his drug addiction.

As he made his way toward his bedroom, he pulled his iPhone out of his pocket to check the time: 2:24 p.m.; he would have to leave for his meeting at Northeastern in about twenty minutes. As he entered his bedroom, his phone began to vibrate in his hand as a call came through from his cousin Chris.

"Hello?" Taylor answered.

"Hey, T," Chris replied. "Do you have a minute?"

"Sure, buddy. What's up?" he asked.

"Are you coming home for Easter this weekend?"

Taylor's heart sank. "I don't think so, man. Sorry."

"I was afraid you were going to say that," Chris replied downheartedly. "Well… my parents are hosting this year, and I just wanted to make sure you knew you were invited. We miss you."

Taylor sighed as he sat down on his bed. "I miss you guys, too."

"Can I be honest with you?"

"Of course," Taylor replied, wondering what was on Chris's mind.

"It's hard to believe you're clean when you don't ever come home."

11

I should have expected that.

"If everything was really fine, I think you'd at least come home for holidays," Chris added.

"I promise that I'm sober," Taylor stated. "Things are just complicated. I would come home if I could."

"But you can," Chris pressed. "Just because you're in a fight with Marc doesn't mean no one else wants to see you. Marc is wrong to blame you for other people's drug problems."

"No, he's not."

"T, you didn't make anyone do anything. If you didn't sell to Luke, I would have found someone else to buy from. Stop blaming yourself for other people's poor decisions."

"The only thing that makes me feel better is the fact that you're sober," Taylor admitted. "I exposed you to terrible things—you and so many other people. You have no idea what it feels like to live with so much shame."

"No, but I have some idea. I used to blame myself for getting my friends into drugs. Most of them, thankfully, are on better paths now, but a lot of damage was done before I sobered up."

"It's small in comparison to the damage I have caused, and you would never have gotten into drugs if I hadn't continuously thrown parties at your house."

"You don't know that," Chris retorted. "My life was missing something, and I thought partying was the answer. I would have gotten into trouble without your help."

"Partying is definitely not the answer."

"No, it's not. Our lives prove that much, but blame is a vicious cycle: you blame yourself for getting me into drugs; I blame myself for getting Jason messed up; Jay blames himself for getting his ex-girlfriend all screwed up; and I'm pretty sure she's living with a lot of self-loathing. It never ends. But we can't keep thinking like that because it's a farce. When you told me that you feel responsible for my issues, it set me free from a significant amount of guilt—but *not* because you are to blame."

Chris's words caught Taylor off guard.

"I never blamed you for my drug problem because I knew I had made the conscious decision to dabble," Chris continued. "The thought of you being responsible for that was preposterous to me, which made me realize I was not responsible for Jason, Jon, or Bryan's past drug use. They all made their own decisions for their own reasons—just like I did."

Taylor was somewhat stunned by the wisdom flowing from his younger cousin's mouth. Recently, every time they spoke, Taylor walked away with a better perspective. The recovery meetings, church, and Bible studies that Chris had been attending since he got sober were changing his life, and that motivated Taylor to attend AA with his father. However, he felt an enormous amount of guilt each time he went because he was still, technically, a drug dealer.

Chris was now seven months sober. He had reached out to Taylor a few months back to share his story. Chris took no credit for his recovery but instead attributed it to the strength he found in God. What he said reminded Taylor of what he had learned at Al-Anon and what his parents had always taught him and his brothers: if you feed your spirit, you will be able to conquer your flesh. Taylor's spirit had been crushed by failure and deep-seeded regret. Numbing his emotions with drugs, instead of facing his problems, had driven him to a very dangerous place.

"You're allowing shame and regret to keep you from coming home, but the truth is every day you remain estranged hurts us more and more," Chris said. "What's done is done. Not coming home only makes the damage worse. Everyone who loves you just wants to forget about the past and move forward with you back in their lives."

Taylor let out a heavy sigh and glanced at the clock on his desk. "I appreciate what you're saying, and I want to come home soon. I really do. I have to head out to a meeting now, but I'll call you tonight, and we can talk more."

"All right. Don't forget," Chris said before ending the call.

As Taylor set down his phone, he dwelled on his cousin's words. He hated the idea of causing his family more pain by keeping to himself, but after realizing the damage he had caused, he had begun to believe everyone would be better off without him. It scared him that he had unwittingly hurt so many people. He was keeping himself away from his family for their own protection. It was a catch twenty-two, though, because protecting them from potential pain was causing them actual pain.

Despite all of the thoughts running through his mind, Taylor knew he had to focus his attention on his academic record before going to his meeting at Northeastern. He sat down at his computer and opened up a PDF file of his transcript. As he looked over his grades, a pit formed in his stomach. He was so embarrassed. How was he going to explain having a 3.4 cumulative GPA through his junior year and then earning a 1.8 average as a senior?

He closed his eyes. *You have to do this*, he said to himself. *You have to try to fix things.*

After opening his eyes, he logged into his bank account online and checked his balance. His father had continued to deposit money into his account to put toward his rent each month, even though Taylor had asked him not to. He did not have the heart to tell his dad that he had made over $50,000 selling drugs and that he did not need any money. He dreaded his family ever finding out how big of a drug dealer he had been.

In November, his father flushed approximately $5,000 worth of drugs down the toilet. Months later, Taylor wished he never let on to how costly the act had been. His father knew nothing about the street value of cocaine or Percocet, and Taylor wished in hindsight that he had kept his mouth shut. He hated taking his father's money, but he was too much of a coward to tell him the truth. The money sitting in Taylor's bank account, safe, storage unit, and safety deposit box did not make up for any of the destruction drugs brought into his life. He would have traded every cent for healthy relationships with his family.

The ironic thing was Taylor did not begin selling drugs to make money. He liked the idea of getting the expensive pills he wanted dirt cheap and being able to sell to his friends at a discount. When he agreed to start dealing, he did so because he wanted to make it easier for people he knew to get their hands on "fun substances" like cocaine, molly, and painkillers. He never imagined how quickly word would spread around campus or how time-consuming dealing drugs would become. Attending class every day and studying were nearly impossible when customers were constantly looking for product. Without football as a motivation to keep his grades high, Taylor quickly lost sight of the big picture. Thoughts such as *why should I go to class to learn about marketing when I'm already a successful salesman?"* motivated him to hit the snooze button far too many mornings, and unfortunately, he did not see the fault in his thought process until his trimester GPA slipped below the allowed minimum.

Failing out of his major was his first wakeup call. His second one came in the form of withdrawal pains—prior to which he had not realized he even had an addiction. Recognizing that he was dependent on a substance horrified him enough to begin detoxing. His final wakeup call was the loss of his relationship with Marc. In fact, Taylor had not touched a painkiller since Marc stormed out of his apartment in November.

After logging out of his computer, Taylor rose from his chair, grabbed his keys, and headed off in his Jeep toward Huntington Avenue. He had feared for months that administrators at Northeastern had heard about his drug abuse, drug-dealing, or both. Therefore, he was surprised to get an email from his former coach earlier that week, checking in on him. He informed Taylor that Northeastern made the shocking decision to terminate its football program and that he would be relocating to another university—location to be determined. He encouraged Taylor to set up a meeting with his advisor to see if he was transfer eligible; he wanted to help Taylor get back on the field and preferably at his new place of employment.

Taylor's father always told him and his brothers that if they did the right thing, God would send the right opportunities their way. Taylor hoped that this was one of those opportunities. He believed he was doing "the right thing" in many areas of his life, but he knew his drug-dealing days had to come to an end if he wanted to move forward. The sickening feeling in his stomach when he sold drugs to Luke that afternoon had only served to solidify that notion.

Chapter 2

Cathy Kagelli and Luke Davids decided to eat lunch at a sushi restaurant one block down from Taylor's South Boston apartment. Although Luke had generously ordered an array of Cathy's favorite dishes, she had no appetite. Her stomach was in knots over the thought of seeing Marc. How was she going to keep from him that she had seen Taylor? She couldn't; her conscience was not going to allow her to do that, and she knew it.

"Why aren't you eating anything?" Luke questioned her as he put down his chopsticks and eyed her in a concerned manner.

"I just don't feel that well," Cathy replied, hoping he wouldn't press the issue.

"Marc didn't get you pregnant, did he?" Luke asked and raised his eyebrows at her expectantly.

Cathy rolled her eyes. "We haven't slept together," she stated in an unamused manner. "Why do you Davids boys always think people who hook up have sex?"

Luke laughed. "Jason and I may have different reasons for assuming that, but I have it on pretty good authority that you're not a virgin."

"I hate you sometimes," Cathy retorted and shook her head.

"Well, if you're not pregnant, then what's wrong with you?" Luke asked curiously.

Cathy assumed he was trying to get her to explain her odd behavior. Unlike Luke, Cathy hated talking about feelings. In their friendship, the female and male roles were a bit reversed: Luke was far more of a "pretty boy" than Cathy was a "girlie girl." Even though Luke was the captain of the varsity hockey team and known for winning fights, Cathy's conversations with him were similar to those had with her girlfriends. She assumed Luke was dying with curiosity over her and

17

Marc's relationship, wanting to know if she was still in love with his brother Jason or if she had truly moved onto Marc. She honestly did not know the answer to that question. Marc was every girl at Montgomery Lake High's dream: a gifted athlete, smart, responsible, and caring, with a body that could be blasted on the cover of magazines and eyes as blue as the sky. However, Jason fit a similar description—at least since he got his life back together.

In the fall, Cathy and Jason went through a disastrous breakup, both hitting their rock bottoms. She had assumed since November that he hated her—until she received a note from him that morning. The letter was still in her pocket, and she looked forward to re-reading it and sorting out her feelings, alone. Luke was eyeing her expectantly, and Cathy knew she had to explain herself in some manner. "I don't want to lie to Marc," she blurted.

"About what?"

"About going to Taylor's!"

"You don't have to lie to him," Luke said, looking puzzled.

Cathy widened her eyes. "Uh, yeah I do unless you want him to find out Taylor sells you drugs."

"You don't have to say anything," Luke stated. "When we pick Marc up at BC, let me do all the talking. He'll ask what we did, and I'll tell him."

"You'll tell him?"

"I'll tell him everything except for the part about Taylor."

Cathy sighed with frustration. "Omitting information like that is not okay! It feels like lying; it puts space between people. My most healthy relationships are my most honest ones. Hiding things from people has brought too much destruction to my life. I am not going to risk losing Marc over this."

Luke let out a heavy breath. "Fine. Tell him. He probably already knows."

"You think?"

Luke shrugged. "He could."

18

"Wouldn't he have confronted you about it?"

"I don't know," Luke replied. "Marc's weird about his family. If he got mad at me about it, people would find out, and that would make Taylor look bad."

"People know he's in a fight with Taylor," Cathy remarked. "That makes Taylor look bad."

Luke shook his head. "It's not the same thing. Brothers fight. Best friends usually don't. Everyone at our school knows Marc and I have a bromance. If we were to stop hanging out, people would notice and talk about it because they love to talk crap."

"Interesting," Cathy said and cocked her head to the side in thought. "Maybe that's why they had a falling out. Maybe Marc found out he was selling drugs to you and stopped talking to him."

"Maybe," Luke replied carelessly. "Like I said, Marc is super protective of his family. He hates Jordan and still doesn't say anything too bad about him."

"Um, other than that he 'tried to date-rape' Michelle Taylor!" Cathy cried, referring to MLH's homecoming queen—Marc's ex-girlfriend, for whom he was presumed to still have some feelings. Marc had not committed to a single girl, including Cathy, since his and Michelle's eighth-grade breakup. He had certainly hooked up with a fair share of girls, but he had called no one but Michelle his girlfriend.

"Everyone knows about what happened between Jordan and Michelle at Chris's house," Luke said matter-of-factly. "That's probably part of the reason why Marc is so weird about his family. He is the only Dunkin with an untarnished reputation."

"Jordan plays for Notre Dame. He's kind of famous," Cathy stated. "Aside from the few who actually believe he tried to date-rape Michelle, I'd say people think pretty highly of him."

"He's a good football player," Luke remarked. "No one will deny that, but I'm talking about what people in our town think. Marc's embarrassed by his brothers' off-field behavior—just like Matt and Jay are embarrassed by me."

Cathy laughed. "Matt's been embarrassed by both of you a million times. I bet he can't wait to go off to college and leave Montgomery."

Luke smirked. "He'll miss me," he said facetiously.

"So, you'd really be okay with me telling Marc that we saw Taylor?" Cathy questioned him.

Luke sighed. "He'll probably take a swing at me, but if keeping it from him is going to tear you up, tell him."

"Thanks," Cathy said, remembering why she adored Luke so much. Even though he was often criticized for being a reckless and spoiled, rich kid, he was as warmhearted as his younger brother.

Chapter 3

Inside his high school's gymnasium, Jason Davids was in a deep conversation with Chantal Kagelli about her identical twin sister Cathy. With added clarity, Jason had numerous regrets about his breakup with Cathy. After much reflection, he realized the root of Cathy's problems was her strained relationship with Chantal. Once having been inseparable, they had been nearly estranged for a year and a half. Jason's relationship with Chantal had also been tarnished for some time. He had erroneously believed Chantal detested him, only to be shocked when she took an interest in helping him climb out of the hole he had dug himself into last fall. Her encouragement had been instrumental in his recovery, leaving him with a strong desire to pay her back in some way.

Jason had honestly believed, for a short time, that Cathy was a monster. It had taken him a while to realize that he and Luke had created that monster and that he had lost the real Cathy months prior to their breakup. He was determined to not only win the love of his life back, but also help restore Cathy and Chantal's relationship.

"Hey! JD! What are you doing stealing my cheerleaders?" Allison Jordan's loud voice projected across the gym, grabbing both Jason and Chantal's full attention.

"Oh, shoot," Chantal said beneath her breath.

"Don't worry; I've got this," Jason assured her as he began waving Ally over to them. Ally was not only the captain of the varsity cheerleading squad, but also his brother Matt's girlfriend.

"Chantal, we can't put up Lisa's stunt without you spotting it," Ally said matter-of-factly upon reaching the bleachers. "What are you doing?"

Jason thought Chantal looked downright frightened. She had recently been pulled up to varsity, so he imagined she was a bit intimidated by Ally.

"I'm sorry," Chantal said, looking like a deer in headlights.

"Have you been crying?" Ally asked, widening her warm brown eyes. "What did you do to her, Jay?"

"She was heading to practice until I upset her," Jason replied. "Take it out on me, not her."

Ally rolled her eyes. "Are you okay to come to practice now?"

Chantal nodded and stood up from the bleachers.

"All right then. Go join the squad by the locker room," Ally commanded. "You owe me, Jay."

He smiled. "See you later," he said, assuming Ally would end up at his house because they had no school the following day. "Chantal, I'll call you after dinner," he yelled as she descended the bleachers.

She turned around briefly and nodded at him before following Ally across the gym.

Jason pulled his phone out of his pocket to ask his brothers for a ride home. He hoped one of them was still at the school, although he had not seen Luke in the halls once all afternoon. *Are either of you still at school? I need a ride,* he typed into his iPhone and hit send on their group text.

He received a reply from Luke a moment later saying, *Sorry in Boston with CK and Marc.* Jason's stomach immediately dropped; Luke was the last person he wanted Cathy spending time with. As much as he loved his gregarious brother, he believed Luke was a terrible influence on her. Moreover, it bothered him to hear about Cathy and Marc's relationship—or whatever they were calling it. Luke seemed to look for opportunities to bring it up to Jason, likely to get under his skin and move him to make up with her.

A few seconds later, a text came through from Matt, saying he was already home but that he could get Jason when he picked up Ally from cheerleading practice. *Thanks,* Jason typed in response, wondering how he had ended up with brothers so incredibly different from one another.

Chapter 4

At four o'clock, Marc trucked across the campus of Boston College with a lot more than football on his mind. To say he was shaken up by Detective Roth's warning about Taylor was an understatement-and-a-half. He was startled to learn that Taylor was in imminent danger and shocked that his family had been investigated. Marc could not believe this had become his reality.

As he headed towards the parking lot where Luke and Cathy were waiting for him, he lost himself in thoughts of Taylor. He could not believe the person he had looked up to for the vast majority of his life had turned into the type of person whom detectives investigated.

The pit in Marc's stomach was large and expanding. The last thing he wanted to do was bring Cathy into any of this mess. However, he had to get the burner phone to Taylor before leaving Boston, which would entail calling Taylor—something he was dreading immensely. Since Taylor's phone could be being monitored by his supplier, Marc knew he could not mention the detectives. Therefore, he would have to pretend to suddenly want to visit his brother, as if everything was okay between them. The idea of being fake turned his stomach sour.

Spotting his red truck across the way, Marc felt some relief. *At least Luke didn't crash it,* he thought. He wondered where Luke had taken Cathy and if they had gotten into any trouble. Marc had been on a mission to rescue Cathy from Taylor's mess since they began hooking up in December. *Now, I have to take her to his apartment? Terrible.* Cathy had no idea that Marc knew of her history with pills or that he blamed his brother for getting her into them. Although Luke had been the one to supply Cathy with benzos and painkillers, Marc blamed Taylor for carelessly selling drugs to him.

Chapter 5

Cathy's stomach fluttered as she watched Marc walk across BC's parking lot towards his truck. She thought he looked disturbed and wondered if something had gone wrong at his meeting. "He looks upset," she said to Luke.

"I'm sure he'll tell us what happened," Luke responded. "You still want to tell him we saw Taylor?"

Cathy sighed. "Not now—not if he's upset."

A moment later, Luke climbed out of the truck and into the backseat to let Marc into the driver's seat. As Marc sat down, he let out a heavy breath. Cathy peered at him nervously, wondering what could have possibly gone wrong with the coaches.

Marc looked over at Cathy and smiled slightly. "How are you guys?" he asked.

"Fine," Cathy replied. She was concerned. Although she hated talking about her own emotions, she had a knack for reading those of others. She sensed that Marc felt anxious, which was strange for someone as collected as him.

"What did you guys do?" Marc questioned them.

"A bunch of stuff," Luke replied immediately. "How was your meeting?"

"Um, everything went great with the coaches," Marc responded, sounding a bit distracted. "I know I made the right decision."

"Then what's wrong? You look upset," Cathy stated and raised her eyebrows at him.

"I need to call my brother," Marc said flatly and took a deep breath.

Cathy's stomach sank. Had he somehow found out that they had visited Taylor?

"Is Jordan coming home for Easter?" Luke questioned him, evidently assuming Marc had meant Jordan.

"Oh, I have no idea," Marc replied. "I haven't talked to him since he left for school. I have to call Taylor."

"What?" Luke asked. "Why?"

Marc again let out a heavy breath. "I want to visit him while we're in Boston."

At that point, Cathy felt like she might throw up.

"You do?" Luke questioned him, sounding just as surprised as Cathy felt.

"Yeah," Marc said. "It's, uh, been too long."

Cathy looked back at Luke and eyed him warily.

Luke lowered his eyebrows and glanced at Marc. "What brought this on, dude?"

"The less you two know, the better," Marc stated. "If we go to his place, you guys can just wait in the truck. I don't want to bring you into his mess."

Cathy swallowed a large lump in her throat, realizing that Marc must have found out something about Taylor during his meeting. She assumed the football coaches knew of Taylor. "Does BC want Taylor to play for them?" she asked.

"No!" Marc cried with a short laugh. "They did years ago, but he's in no shape to be back on the field. I just found something out today that made me want to reach out to him while we're in the city; that's all."

Cathy's eyes widened, and her stomach immediately dropped as a sickening thought entered her mind: if Marc was going to visit Taylor, then he would need Taylor's new address. Surely, he would recognize it as a previous location once he punched it into his GPS. Cathy's throat went dry, and she wondered if Luke had the same thought.

"I'm going to call him now to see if he's home," Marc said before picking up his cell phone. "My dad said he moved, and I have no idea where his new place is."

Cathy looked back at Luke, whose eyes were as wide as could be. She could tell he was trying to come up with a plan.

"Marc—" Cathy began.

"Hold on a sec," Marc cut her off with the phone to his ear. "I have to leave a voicemail; he's not answering… Hey, Taylor. It's Marc. I'm in the city today and wanted to come by and see you. Call me back if you're around. Thanks."

Chapter 6

After getting off the phone with Taylor, Chris spent some time brainstorming possible ways to get him to come home. He wanted to believe that Taylor was sober, but sober people usually spent time with their families. If Taylor was keeping himself away from them, even on holidays, then he was likely hiding something. After some time, he decided to call Jordan to see if he could offer any insight into what had been going on with Taylor.

"Hey, Little D!" Jordan greeted him as cheerfully as usual. "What's up?"

"Are you coming home this weekend?" Chris asked.

"You bet!" Jordan exclaimed. "I'm actually at the airport, getting on my plane in about an hour."

"Nice!" Chris stated excitedly. "I'm so happy to hear that, dude. Have you talked to Taylor at all?"

"A little," Jordan replied. "I want to visit him tomorrow."

"Try to talk him into coming to my house on Easter," Chris said.

"That's my plan."

"I'm so glad you're coming home. I thought you might be going away with your friends for spring break."

"I considered it, but there are more important things for me to take care of back home," Jordan remarked.

"Taylor told me he's clean now," Chris said.

"I heard. I'm pumped. I want to see it with my own eyes."

"I do, too. I miss him."

"You and me both, buddy," Jordan stated. "My plane lands around ten tonight. My parents are picking me up. I'm sure they'll fill me in on what's been going on with Taylor a bit more than he has."

"He hasn't come home at all. That sits weird with me," Chris admitted.

"He hasn't? My dad said he's been sober for a few months."

"That's what I heard too, but the only people who have seen him are your parents."

"Well, my dad said Marc and Taylor had a falling out, so maybe he just doesn't want to see Marc. That kid holds grudges like no other."

"I have a feeling it's more than that," Chris said. "Do whatever you can to get him to come home."

"Will do," Jordan pledged. "See you soon, buddy."

"Later," Chris said before ending the call. He was relieved that Jordan had chosen coming home over going away for spring break. Jordan had an impressive football season, and Chris knew that his priorities were finally in the right place. He wished Marc would ask Michelle to tell him the truth about the date-rape incident instead of erroneously assuming Jordan had slipped something into her drink. Chris missed his cousins being close with each other.

A few moments later, Chris received a call from Jason. As soon as he saw his best friend's name appear on the screen, he became curious to hear if Jason had talked to Cathy. Chris's thoughts were all over the place in regard to her. He adored the girl she had once been, and he was hopeful that Marc would help her find herself again. He feared Jason would get in the way of that. As great of a place as Jason was in personally, Cathy was his weakness. "What's up?" Chris spoke into his phone.

"Just waiting for Matt to pick me up at school," Jason replied.

"Why are you still at school?"

"I stayed after to talk to Chantal about Cathy. Did you know she thought Cathy pretended to be her and broke up with Jon?"

"I thought the same thing," Chris stated flatly.

"What?!"

"She didn't?"

"My God. You guys all think she is the devil. No, she didn't pretend to be Chantal; Jon mistook a message Cathy left him as being from Chantal."

"Huh?"

"The day Chantal and Jon broke up, Cathy left him a message, saying how upset she was with his behavior and that it looked like he should be dating Alyssa because he was spending all his time with her. Jon thought it was from Chantal—same phone number, same voice—and took it as a breakup. That's why he flipped out on Chantal and said he was going to date Alyssa when she called him later that day. That's why they both thought they had been dumped."

"What?!" Chris cried, widening his eyes. Everything Jason said blew his mind. It made too much sense not to be true. "And you know this *how*?"

Jason sighed. "I've known for over a year," he admitted. "Lisa and Cathy figured it out, somehow."

"Why didn't you guys tell anyone?"

"Cathy wanted to, but Lisa and I convinced her not to tell Chantal because we were afraid she'd get back together with Jon."

Chris dropped his jaw. "He is going to kill you when he finds out about this."

"Yeah," Jason agreed. "I know."

"Holy crap! So, Cathy's not really a manipulative psycho who enjoys seeing her sister brokenhearted?"

"No!" Jason cried. "She was trying to protect Chantal from Jon. Jon's great now, but back then he was toxic. You guys honestly believed Cathy did that? You thought I was dating a psychopath?"

Chris laughed. "It all makes so much sense now. I thought you knew she broke them up and just didn't care because you were mad at Jon. At one point, I even thought you had put her up to it."

"Chris!" Jason exclaimed.

"I'm sorry, dude, but the whole thing made no sense. I knew Jon and Chantal weren't liars, so something wasn't right."

"Yeah, well now I understand why you all hate my ex-girlfriend and why Alyssa turned on Cathy… and why everyone Chantal is close with thinks Cathy is insane."

"Well, to be fair, she went a little crazy," Chris stated, recalling Jason and Cathy's breakup.

"That's my fault," Jason stated dryly. "You know it is," he added.

Chris wondered if Jason would ever be able to forgive himself for introducing Cathy to prescription drugs. In Chris's eyes, Jason was not to blame for Cathy's drug use; Cathy was. Although Jason, Luke, and Taylor all played roles in Cathy apprehending the pills, she made her own choices. Chris tried to remember what Cathy was like before Xanax got a grip on her. Although his memory was a bit foggy, he could recall thinking she was perfect for Jason: caring, fun, and witty. In hindsight, however, Chris could see that Jason and Cathy were more of a perfect storm than a perfect couple. Although their breakup did not take place until the fall of ninth grade, their storm began brewing one year prior. Chris was amazed that it took so long to see the tempest coming.

Chapter 7

18 Months Prior – September of 2016

After parking his truck on South Huntington Street in the Jamaica Plain neighborhood of Boston, Marc glanced over at Luke, who was sitting shotgun. "No matter how crazy things get tonight, remember we have to wake up to tailgate in the morning. Taylor's crew parties hard. If they offer to take us out, don't do anything stupid."

Luke laughed. "Like what?"

"Like go back to some girl's dorm or blow lines of cocaine."

Luke widened his eyes. "I've never even seen coke, and what college girl would want *me*?"

"A drunk one," Marc replied. "Girls love you. Don't be stupid."

Luke smirked. "When the girls hear you're Taylor Dunkin's brother, they're going to be all over you. Your brother is 'the big man on campus' around here. Take your own advice, Marky Marc."

Marc rolled his eyes. "Let's just go inside," he said before climbing out of the truck.

A moment later when Taylor opened the door to let Marc and Luke into his apartment, Marc was surprised to see his brother wearing sweatpants and a t-shirt. "It's only seven o'clock. Are you going to bed already?" Marc asked as he placed his bag of clothes down on the kitchen floor. A handful of Taylor's friends, Taylor's girlfriend Julie, and a few other girls were sitting around the kitchen table, playing a card game. Everyone looked dressed up for a party.

"I have a game tomorrow," Taylor replied and picked Marc's bag up off the floor. "I'll be asleep by eight."

Marc lowered his eyebrows. "Your game's not 'til 3:30."

"Little bro, I have a whole morning ritual before my games," Taylor stated and motioned for Marc and Luke to follow him into his bedroom. "I don't ever go out the night before a game."

"Then why did you invite us up here tonight?" Marc asked as he followed Taylor into his room.

"Oh, you guys will have a great time," Taylor assured them after tossing Marc's bag onto his bed. "Ryan and Julie are going to take you to a party over on Columbus Ave."

"Nice," Luke sang and dropped his backpack to the floor.

"You guys are going to sleep on my living room couch," Taylor informed them. "It pulls out into a bed. I'll put your bags and some sheets and pillows out there after everyone leaves. Ryan is bringing the keg to the party, so he promised he'd be there by seven-thirty. You'll be leaving with him in a few minutes. Have you eaten dinner yet?"

"No," Marc replied.

Taylor pointed to the door. "There's pizza on the counter. Eat a bunch of slices if you plan on drinking. I don't want to wake up to the sound of either one of you puking later."

"Neither one of us usually drinks," Marc retorted.

"Well, I'm sure you will tonight, so fill up on carbs before you go," Taylor said matter-of-factly. "And if you don't have an alcohol tolerance, don't touch any hard liquor. Please. The last thing I need is for Mom and Dad to show up to tailgate and see you two hungover."

"Mom, Dad, and Chris aren't picking us up until eleven," Marc said. "We'll be fine."

"All right. Good deal," Taylor remarked. "Go eat," he added and nodded toward the kitchen.

After eating a few slices of pepperoni pizza, Marc walked around the apartment, counting the number of framed newspaper articles hanging on the walls. They were each about a different football record Taylor broke or an award he won. Many articles featured pictures of him from Pop Warner, high school, and college. *You're a star, bro*, Marc thought as he counted the twenty-third frame. He locked his eyes on the article, which was from Northeastern's newspaper. In May, the paper had published a feature on Taylor with information about his upbringing, hometown, and accolades. Skimming the paragraphs, Marc saw his own name mentioned a few times. He wondered if any girls at the party would care that he was Taylor's brother. He had never before attended a college party, despite partying many times at Chris's house with Taylor's friends. Regardless of how well he knew Ryan, Julie, and most of their crew, Marc felt strange going out without his brother.

An hour later, Marc and Luke were in the midst of the party, surrounded by kids who honestly did not look much older than them. Ryan poured Luke and Marc beers from the keg, and Julie introduced them to some of her sorority sisters. The girls were surprised to hear that Marc and Luke were so young. Marc had anticipated that their ages would turn girls off from talking to him and Luke, but he was wrong. Hearing that Marc was Taylor's brother was enough to keep their interest.

"Your brother's going to be famous when he gets out of here," a pretty brunette named Kelly said. "I just hope he takes Julie along for the ride."

Marc smiled. "He'd be stupid not to. Julie's great."

"She is," Kelly remarked. "Our sorority wants her to run for Homecoming Queen. She'd win just because she's Taylor's girlfriend. Everyone knows her."

"Is she going to run?" Marc asked.

"I don't think so," Kelly replied and shook her head. "She doesn't like being the center of attention."

"Obviously," Luke stated with a short laugh. "How could she ever be the center of attention when she's always with Taylor? The spotlight is on him and him alone."

Kelly and her friend Jessica both laughed. "Good point, sophomore in high school," Kelly teased Luke. "What's your story?"

"I don't have a story," Luke replied nonchalantly. "I'm just here because we're going to the game tomorrow."

"It should be a good game. If we win, tomorrow night's party will be much bigger than this one," Jessica said. "You should stick around for that," she added in a playful tone.

"Okay. I'll try," Luke agreed and spread his lips into a crooked smile.

Marc was not even surprised that Jessica, a nineteen-year-old blonde with large breasts and a stunning smile was flirting with Luke. Despite being just shy of sixteen, Luke was arguably the best-looking guy at the party.

"Marc! Luke! Come over here!" Ryan called from across the living room by the beer pong table.

"Oh, boy," Kelly sang in a mischievous tone. "Ryan's going to try to spice up your night."

"Huh?" Marc asked.

Kelly laughed and then looked at Jessica. "We'll see you guys around."

Jessica smiled. "Bye, Luke," she said and squeezed his shoulder.

Marc smirked at Luke before heading over toward Ryan.

"You guys are welcome to sign up for the tournament," Ryan offered once they reached his side. "I'm not playing tonight because my usual partner is in bed like a wuss, but I think someone should keep the Dunkin beer pong legacy going."

"Oh. I've got nothing on Taylor," Marc stated immediately. "I would embarrass my family name if I played."

Ryan laughed. "Well, what else do you guys want to do? I promised Taylor you'd have a good time. Do you want some molly or something?"

Marc raised his eyebrows and widened his eyes.

"Molly? As in MDMA?" Luke questioned him.

"Yeah, ecstasy," Ryan replied matter-of-factly. "My friend Rob has plenty of it to go around tonight."

"Taylor told me you guys don't roll anymore," Marc said, wondering if his brother had lied to him.

"*Taylor* doesn't roll," Ryan clarified. "Julie hates drugs. He gave it all up for her and football."

Marc couldn't help but wonder what "all" entailed, but he didn't want to press Ryan on the subject. He was just happy to hear that Julie was a good influence on his brother. They had been dating for roughly six months. She was a sweet southern belle from South Carolina, and Marc's family adored her.

"I'll try molly," Luke said nonchalantly.

"Luke!" Marc exclaimed and turned toward his friend. "You can't do that!"

"Why not?" Luke asked. "Ryan offered it to us; I have money; there are no parents around; and we're spending the night at Taylor's. It sounds like the perfect time to try it."

Marc's heart began to pound against his chest, and he immediately regretted inviting Luke to Boston. "No," Marc stated sternly. "We have to be up in the morning. Molly will keep you awake all night long."

"That *is* true," Ryan agreed. "You won't get much sleep if you roll, and you'll feel like crap at the game, but—and this is a big 'but'— you'll feel pretty $%#@ awesome tonight."

Luke laughed. "I want to try it. Let's do it."

"You are out of your mind," Marc said in a frustrated tone. "If you touch that crap, you're on your own."

"I'm confident in my ability to get back to Taylor and Ryan's apartment," Luke stated assuredly.

"Good, because if you take molly, I'm hopping on the Green Line," Marc said matter-of-factly.

"You're going to leave?" Luke questioned him.

"I have no interest in being around you while you're all cuddly and emotionally expressive," Marc retorted.

Ryan laughed. "That's what the girls are for."

"You're such a pussy!" Luke exclaimed and shook his head at Marc. "Live a little."

"Do whatever you want," Marc stated flatly. "I'm going to check on Julie." Although he assumed everyone would show her respect, he still felt obligated to look after her in Taylor's absence.

Julie was easy to find; she was sitting at the kitchen table surrounded by the girls who had been at Taylor's apartment. "Hi, Marc!" she cried brightly as their eyes met.

"Hey," he greeted her with a warm smile.

She jumped up from her seat and motioned for him to sit down. "Take my seat. I can sit on your lap."

Marc widened his eyes before letting out a short laugh. "Um, okay," he said and sat down at the table.

Julie hopped onto his lap and threw her slender arm around his shoulders. "Guys, doesn't Marc look like Taylor?" she asked as she rested her head against his.

All of the girls nodded.

"Yeah, except I'm three inches shorter and about fifty pounds lighter," Marc admitted.

"You're adorable," Julie remarked. "Isn't he?" she questioned her friends.

Marc was sure he was blushing bright red when all the girls nodded and smiled at him. He assumed Julie was trying to make him feel comfortable. She reminded him of his ex-girlfriend Michelle, aside from her blonde hair and southern accent.

"Where's your friend?" a redhead named Meghan asked.

"He's hanging out with Ryan," Marc replied carelessly.

"He's cute," Meghan stated. "I can't believe you guys are in high school. You look older than most of the freshmen we see around here."

"That's because every Dunkin boy begins working out at age ten," Julie said. "You should see their cousin Chris. He's, like, thirteen but just as built as Marc. I thought he was at least sixteen when I met him."

"Chris definitely looks and acts older than he is," Marc agreed. "He's coming to the game tomorrow with my parents."

"He's adorable, too, but *definitely* off limits, girls," Julie said facetiously and winked at her friends. "Marc, you're almost seventeen, though, right?"

Marc nodded. "Next month."

"Well, I just turned eighteen last month," a girl named Samantha said and locked her brown eyes on Marc. "See, you're not *that* young."

"Well, that makes me feel better," Marc responded. He could not deny he was enjoying the girls' attention. It certainly helped quell the frustration he felt after talking to Luke and Ryan.

"We're about to play Circle of Death," Julie said. "Do you want in?"

"Sure," Marc agreed with a shrug.

"Do you know how to play?" Julie asked.

Marc nodded. "I think Taylor and Jordan have taught me how to play every drinking game they know."

Julie laughed. "Sam, ask Matt to bring a pitcher of beer over here from the keg," she said and nodded toward Samantha. "He said that he and Josh wanted to play."

Sam immediately stood up from her seat and walked across the kitchen to a group of guys huddled around the kegerator.

"Sam's pledging our sorority, so she gets to run our errands tonight," Julie explained. "She's the only freshmen we invited to the party, so she's pretty excited to be here."

Marc locked his eyes on Sam, who had loosely-curled, long brown hair, a thin waist, and long legs. *She's cute*, he decided, wondering if she had any interest in getting to know him better.

"You should talk to her, Marc," Meghan prompted.

Marc felt his cheeks redden.

"Don't you have a girlfriend?" Julie questioned him.

Marc shook his head.

"You're not going out with that gorgeous brunette who came to Taylor's last game with you?" Julie pressed, referring to Michelle.

Marc shook his head again. "She's one of my best friends, but we're not together. We dated a few years ago."

"Taylor likes her for you," Julie said.

"I know," Marc remarked. "Everyone does, but relationships complicate things, and we're happy as friends."

"Well, then you have permission to hook up with any of my single friends," Julie announced playfully.

Marc smiled as Sam made her way back to the table with a couple of guys trailing behind her. Taylor's close friend Matt McSweeney set a fresh pitcher of beer down on the table. "What's up, Marc?" he greeted him in a friendly tone. "Good to see you, buddy."

"Good to see you," Marc responded.

"Are there any more chairs?" Taylor's friend Josh Swanson asked from behind Matt.

"Why don't we just follow Marky Marc's lead and let the girls sit on our laps?" Matt suggested.

"Done!" Meghan cried and stood up from her seat. She motioned for her other friend Heather, who was sitting opposite Marc, to do the same. Marc could not help but wonder about the hookup history within Taylor's group of friends. Both Matt and Josh were good-looking kids, so Marc could understand why the girls wanted to share seats with them. Meghan sat down on Matt's lap and Heather sat on Josh's. Sam was the only one sitting by herself.

"Sam, trade places with me!" Julie cried out brightly.

Sam lowered her perfectly shaped eyebrows. "Why?" she asked.

"So, I can have my own seat," Julie replied immediately—although Marc assumed she wanted him and Sam to get better acquainted.

"Whatever you say, VP," Sam replied before swapping places with Julie, who was the vice president of their sorority. "Do you care?" she questioned Marc before sitting down.

Marc laughed. "Not if you don't," he replied with a flirtatious smirk.

Sam smiled back at him and then positioned herself on his lap. She was wearing sweet smelling perfume, which only increased his attraction towards her. *I think this night may turn out all right, after all,* he concluded.

***

Around nine o'clock the following morning, Marc creased his blue eyes open after hearing Taylor's voice coming from the kitchen. He turned to his right to see Samantha sleeping beside him. Peering around the living room, he realized Luke was nowhere to be found. Marc widened his eyes and sat up straight. Without waking up Sam, he made his way into the kitchen to see if Taylor knew anything about Luke's whereabouts.

Taylor smiled widely when Marc entered the room. "Good morning, Casanova," he greeted him with a short laugh. "Sixteen years old and already bringing home sorority girls? Maybe you take more after Jordan than you think."

Marc laughed. "Have you heard anything from Luke?" he asked.

Taylor nodded. "He's asleep in my room. He got in around eight and looked like he had a rough night—not in a bad way, but in a rough way."

"In a 'rolling on ecstasy' way?" Marc inquired.

"Exactly."

"He's an idiot."

Taylor shrugged. "Just let him sleep for a few hours, and he'll be okay for the game. I'm heading out to breakfast with Julie. Do you want to come?"

"I don't want to leave Samantha asleep in your living room," Marc replied. "I'll go back to bed for a bit and just eat at the tailgate."

"All right," Taylor said and held up his hand to pound Marc's. "Maybe I'll see you when I get back. If not, tell Mom and Dad I'll meet up with you guys after the game. I think they said something about reservations at the Capital Grille."

Marc pounded Taylor back and said, "You got it," before heading into the living room.

Sam woke up when Marc climbed back into bed. "Hi," she greeted him in a sleepy tone. "Why are you up so early?"

"Oh, I was just talking to Taylor in the kitchen. He's heading out to breakfast with Julie."

Sam smiled. "I think we were up a lot later than either one of them."

Marc laughed. "That's your fault," he said lightheartedly.

She smiled again. "You didn't complain."

Marc blushed before leaning in to kiss her.

"Do we have the place to ourselves?" she asked.

"Taylor's about to walk out the door; Luke's passed out in Taylor's room; and I have no idea if Ryan's home," Marc replied.

Sam raised her eyebrows and eyed him flirtatiously. "I can be quiet if you can be quiet."

Marc smiled widely and pulled her slender body on top of his. Although he doubted a relationship would develop between them, considering that he was still in high school, he could not deny that they had chemistry. He finally understood how Jordan had pulled off losing his virginity to a hot sophomore in college when he was only sixteen; being Taylor Dunkin's brother certainly had its perks.

Chapter 8

Many hours later, after a fun afternoon of tailgating with his parents, Chris, Julie, and some of Taylor's friends, Marc was sitting in the waiting room at Brigham and Women's Hospital in disbelief that such a great day could end so badly. Luke, who had finally shown up at the football game during the second quarter, was sitting beside Marc, attempting to nap. Chris was on the other side of Luke, flipping through a *Sports Illustrated* magazine. Taylor, his parents, and Julie were inside the emergency room, waiting for MRI results.

During the third quarter of the game, Taylor had attempted a rushing touchdown to take the lead when a defensive player made a low hit to keep him from reaching the end zone. When Taylor hit the ground, his leg landed in an unnatural position, and the groan he let out could be heard from the stands. As every Northeastern player and coach rushed over to Taylor, Marc watched his father's eyes fill with tears. His father had played wide receiver at University of Miami in the early 1990s, and he knew more about the game than anyone Marc had ever met. In fact, he had even coached at the junior college level when Marc was a child. Mr. Dunkin had seen terrible career-ending injuries as both a player and a coach, so Marc knew by his father's reaction that Taylor's season was likely in jeopardy.

As Marc sat in the waiting room, he tried to imagine the thoughts going through his brother's mind. This was Taylor's *senior* season. Although he was enrolled in a five-year program with co-op and eligible to play the following year, Taylor needed both years on the field to gain the exposure needed to be drafted by the NFL.

Twenty minutes later, Marc's mother and Julie entered the waiting room, both looking despondent.

"How is he?" Marc asked as soon as they were within hearing distance.

Julie dropped her hazel eyes to the floor and shook her head sadly.

"It appears as though he tore his ACL, MCL, and both menisci," Mrs. Dunkin replied.

"What?!" Marc shrieked. "How?"

"He thinks he might have damaged his menisci during practice, which is why his ACL and MCL tore so easily," Mrs. Dunkin said. "He admitted to having some knee pain before the game but resolving to play through it."

Marc scowled. "He's competitive to a fault."

Marc's mother sighed. "He's devastated. His season's over. Your father's trying to calm him down."

"He's going to need surgery, right?" Marc inquired.

His mother nodded. "They're going to keep him overnight, and he'll meet with an orthopedic surgeon tomorrow morning. Physical therapy before surgery is an option, but Taylor wants to get back on the field, so he's pushing for surgery as soon as possible."

Marc let out a heavy breath. "Will he be okay to play next year?"

Marc's mother shrugged. "Sorry, honey. We don't have many answers right now. Before we start speculating about next year, we have to figure out who's going to care for him after his surgery, if he needs to move back home, and if he has to take a medical leave of absence from school."

"I can help take care of him," Julie offered. "He's not going to want to miss school. He's the most driven person I know."

"Thanks, sweetheart," Mrs. Dunkin said and placed a supportive hand on Julie's shoulder. "It's good that you're a nursing major and that he has you in his life. Between you and our family, we should be able to work everything out."

"Can we go see him?" Chris asked.

"You don't want to see him like this," Mrs. Dunkin replied. "He's not in the right mind. I think they're going to sedate him if your father can't calm him down."

Marc cringed at the sound of his mother's words. He imagined it felt to Taylor like his dreams were slipping through his fingers.

Chapter 9

Between September and February, a lot transpired in the lives of Chris, Taylor, Luke, Cathy, and Jason. Taylor underwent knee surgery, opted to stay in school, and remained in Boston where Julie could help take care of him. However, because he had a stage III ACL tear there were some complications, which led to a second surgery. Despite having the support of his girlfriend, family, and friends, Taylor grew incredibly discouraged. Northeastern ended up having a losing football season, and Taylor carried the blame on his shoulders. Without being a part of the team, he felt lost.

In the meantime, Luke had remained in contact with Ryan and his friend Rob Anuzelli who sold molly. Through Rob, he was able to get any substance he wanted. It did not take long for Luke to extend the offer to Chris.

Chris took an interest in trying a variety of drugs, pledging not to do any of them enough to form an addiction. In October, he convinced Jason to eat mushrooms with him, which stunned Cathy. She could not believe her level-headed boyfriend would engage in such risky behavior. Jason told her that he was bored and just felt like experimenting. Because mushrooms were natural, he did not consider them "drugs." This gave her an uneasy feeling, and she began to view Chris as a bad influence in Jason's life.

During a party at Chris's house later that month, Jason was "bored" enough to eat a pot brownie. Afterwards, he researched the medicinal properties of marijuana and sent Cathy a plethora of information on how weed could treat anxiety. He wanted her to try it—not to get high—to see if it made her feel any better. Anxiety and depression had been plaguing her since she lost Chantal's friendship. Cathy read up on marijuana for weeks before agreeing to try it. Knowing it was not physically addictive, she perceived no harm in seeing if it placated her anxiety. So, at Chris's next party, she ate a weed cookie. The effect took nearly two hours to kick in, but when it did, she felt more relaxed than she had all month.

Edibles were not easy to come by, but Luke could get Jason as much marijuana as he wanted. Chris's house could be used as a bakery when his parents traveled for work, but cookies only stayed fresh for a few days, and they could not be stored in plain sight. It was not long before Cathy and Jason realized smoking weed would be much more convenient.

By January, Luke no longer had to go through Rob to get drugs. Taylor offered him a much better deal. Luke was shocked that Taylor was willing to sell to him, but nevertheless, he appreciated the steep discount. Hoping to quell Cathy's anxiety, Luke began offering her pills. The idea of taking any prescription drug freaked her out, so Jason offered to try everything first. He was not a fan of the way Xanax or Klonopin made him feel, but they both helped ease Cathy's overactive mind. Luke seemingly had a limitless supply of these pills, and he never charged her for anything. Jason and Cathy viewed their experimental drug use as trying to treat an illness, and Cathy did not believe she was doing anything immoral. She simply wanted to numb the sadness she felt every day without Chantal in her life so she could focus on being a good friend, girlfriend, and student.

Despite Cathy's best friend Lisa's initial stance against marijuana, Cathy convinced her to try it. Lisa had developed an aversion to alcohol after her father's fatal accident; however, she ended up liking the calming effects of marijuana. This helped her rekindle her friendship with Chris, and Cathy hoped they would get back together. However, when Lisa had been avoiding Chris, she had hooked back up with Jeff Brooke—one of Andy's friends whom she had kissed before she met Chris. As a result, there was a lot of talk circulating about Lisa and Jeff becoming an official couple.

February of 2017

"I think I might start letting Jeff call me his girlfriend," Lisa said one afternoon while getting ready at Cathy's for a gathering at Chris's house later that evening. He had only invited Cathy, Lisa, and Jason, likely in hopes of hooking back up with Lisa.

"Really?" Cathy asked while applying a thick coat of black mascara to her long eyelashes. "But I don't know him well enough for him to be your boyfriend," she protested facetiously.

"We've been hooking up since, like, October," Lisa reminded her. "He hasn't hooked up with anyone else, so he's clearly loyal. The fact that I haven't let him call me his girlfriend—per your advice—has kept him more interested. I think."

"Then why let him now?"

Lisa shrugged.

Cathy smirked. "I know you better than that. Why do you want him to be your boyfriend *now*?"

Lisa sent Cathy a playful glare. "There are some *things* I want to do with him that I would only do with a boyfriend."

Cathy started laughing. "You whore!"

Lisa laughed. "Actually, by becoming his girlfriend, I would be preventing people from thinking that."

"You want to get in his pants?"

Lisa giggled. "Not necessarily, but I want to at least let him in mine."

Cathy widened her eyes. "Definitely don't do that unless he's your boyfriend. I can't be best friends with a slut."

Lisa playfully slapped Cathy. "I'll keep that in mind," she said and turned to look at her reflection in Cathy's full-length mirror. "Then in the back of my mind, there's always Chris," she nonchalantly said a few seconds later.

"If you're not over Chris, then you shouldn't go out with Jeff," Cathy stated immediately. "For the sake of all three of you."

"Does *anyone* ever *really* get over their first love?" Lisa asked.

"I'm not sure; I've only had one," Cathy replied.

"A part of you will love Jay for the rest of your life," Lisa commented assuredly.

Cathy shifted her weight awkwardly and then sat down on her bed. "Is it naïve to believe that he could be my only love?"

Lisa laughed. "Yes. When you get to high school, the older boys are going to want to date you, and all the girls in our grade will be vying for Jay's attention because it will be the first time he's attended public school since kindergarten."

Cathy's stomach sank as her facial expression fell. "You think because he won't be at an all-boys school, he'll meet someone he likes better than me?"

Lisa shook her head and sat down next to Cathy. "No. I think you and Jay share a connection strong enough to keep his eyes on you; *you've* just got to keep your eyes on him."

At that moment, Cathy could not imagine Jason ever losing her attention. "You know, Chris never meant to choose Jon's feelings over yours," she said offhandedly. "Don't you think it might be worth trying to work things out with him?" she pressed.

Lisa fell back onto Cathy's neatly made bed and sighed. "Maybe. I just don't think I want to enter high school as Chris Dunkin's girlfriend."

Cathy darted her green eyes at Lisa in confusion. "What's wrong with being his girlfriend?"

Lisa pushed herself further up on the bed and rested her back against Cathy's decorative pillows. She crossed her legs and then planted her cat-like eyes on Cathy. "I'm not one to care about reputations—at all—but he's got one worth caring about."

Cathy lowered her eyebrows in confusion. "Everyone loves Chris."

Lisa let out a short sigh and then smiled at Cathy. "I know they do."

"So, what's the problem?"

Lisa looked down at her purple fingernails. "I just think I'd rather date the class president than the class party planner—that's all."

Cathy dropped her jaw. "You want to date Andy?!" she exclaimed, referring to her twin sister's boyfriend.

Lisa started laughing hysterically. "No!" she shrieked. "I was being metaphorical! C'mon, Kagelli! You're smarter than that!"

"Then why are you coming with me to Chris's tonight?"

Lisa smiled. "Well, we're not freshmen yet."

Chapter 10

Around dinnertime, Jason's brother Matt dropped Jason, Cathy, and Lisa off at Chris's house. Cathy's mother was planning to pick the girls up at ten-thirty. During the drive to Chris's, Cathy wondered if it would be awkward to hang out as a foursome. Chris and Lisa had hung out a few times that month, but it had been in a large group setting.

"My parents won't be home until after midnight, and my little sister is sleeping over her friend's house," Chris said after Jason, Lisa, and Cathy settled down in his living room. "House to ourselves!"

"Sweet," Jason said from beside Cathy on the loveseat.

Lisa, who was sitting beside Chris on the couch, looked a bit stiff. The sexual tension between them was apparent, which made Cathy uncomfortable. After her talk with Lisa earlier, she did not want Chris to get his hopes up about getting back together with her. If they did hook back up, would Lisa really break up with him before high school? Could she truly be that cold?

"So, I was thinking that we smoke a bowl and then order pizza," Chris said with a childlike grin.

"I can see you've put a lot of thought into the evening," Lisa commented sarcastically and playfully nudged him.

Jason darted his eyes at Cathy, likely surprised that Lisa was already flirting with Chris.

"Or if you don't want to smoke, we have another option," Chris added and raised his eyebrows.

"Like what? Did Luke get you edibles?" Jason asked.

"No," Chris replied and shook his head. "Jay, come upstairs with me for a second."

Cathy glanced at Chris suspiciously, wondering what he was trying to hide from the girls. Obviously, Jason would tell her everything that happened.

49

"O-kay," Jason replied with hesitation and then followed Chris upstairs.

"That's weird," Lisa said as she stood up from the couch and walked over to the loveseat. She sat down beside Cathy and lowered her eyebrows. "What do you think he has upstairs?"

Cathy shrugged. "No clue."

"Well, whatever it is, do you think Jay will do it?"

"It depends on what it is. He has no problem turning Chris down. He doesn't even drink."

"What does Jay have against alcohol again?"

"I think he avoids it because of me; he knows it would make me uncomfortable if he drank. He used to say his brothers would kill him, but Luke and Matt both drink now, so that excuse doesn't work anymore," Cathy replied.

"Yeah, and now Luke deals drugs," Lisa stated dryly.

Cathy took a deep breath. "I'm so worried he's going to get in trouble. It's great because he gives us weed and stuff, but if he ever got caught, his parents would be devastated."

"What other 'stuff' has he been giving you?" Lisa asked and locked eyes with Cathy.

Cathy looked down at her hands. "Just stuff for me to take when I get bad anxiety."

"Like?"

Cathy glanced at up Lisa, positive that she looked ashamed. "No one knows except for Jason and Luke."

"Cathy, what did he give you?" Lisa pressed, sounding concerned.

Cathy sighed. "It's really not a big deal. He gives me anxiety meds, like Xanax and Klonopin."

Lisa widened her green eyes. "Cath," she said and let out a heavy breath. "That stuff is bad news. Xanax is really addictive."

"I know," Cathy stated defensively. "That's why I don't take it often. I just have it in case I need it."

"A year ago, we were both against drugs," Lisa said quietly and looked away from Cathy.

"We still are," Cathy commented flatly. "Neither one of us even drinks. I'm just taking medication that I would be prescribed if I were an adult."

"Jason was against drugs, too," Lisa added.

"He's only trying to find ways to help me deal with my anxiety and depression," Cathy assured her. "Jay hates the way benzos make him feel. He likes weed and mushrooms because in his eyes they're not drugs; they're food."

"You see it though, right? Don't you get it?" Lisa asked and searched Cathy's eyes. Cathy assumed she was referring to why she did not want to be linked to Chris when she started high school. "I still love Chris," Lisa admitted, "but he's messed up, and I need someone stable because I'm susceptible."

"I get it," Cathy replied, realizing that it was not Lisa's cold-heartedness but rather her wisdom preventing her from getting back together with Chris.

"So, I'm going to make the best of tonight, and then that's it for me and Chris," Lisa said quietly. "It has to be."

A few moments later, Jason came downstairs without Chris and sat down on the couch. Cathy thought he looked agitated. "Lisa, Chris wants you to go upstairs and talk to him," he said and nodded toward her.

"Me? Why?" Lisa asked, eyeing him warily.

Jason took a deep breath. "Just go talk to him," he stated rather downheartedly and pointed toward the stairs.

"What a quick way to get me back into his bedroom," Lisa muttered while walking across the living room towards the grand bridal staircase.

"What did you guys do?" Cathy immediately questioned Jason, sending him a concerned look.

He moved from the couch and sat down next to her on the loveseat. She held her gaze on him. He placed his hand on her shoulder and looked her directly in the eye. "I didn't do anything."

"What did he want you to do?"

Jason sighed. "Drink something spiked with something he got from my brother."

Cathy raised her eyebrows. "Luke got him alcohol?"

Jason shook his head. "No. It's a powder that you can put in a drink, and it gives you energy."

"Oh, well, that sounds less harmful than what I was expecting to hear," Cathy commented. "Although, you look a little upset about it."

"I just don't know why he can't hang out *one night* without getting messed up," Jason expressed in a frustrated manner.

"Did you guys have an argument?"

"I asked him not to drink it so we could have a chill night, but he said he would leave it up to Lisa."

"So, Lisa and Chris might come downstairs super energized in a few minutes?"

"No. It takes longer than a few minutes to kick in. If they get weird, we can leave."

Cathy rested her head on Jason's shoulder. "She's not going to get back together with him. She thinks he's a bad influence on her."

"Well, tonight will prove that—one way or another."

Cathy hoisted herself onto Jason's lap and looked into his eyes. "You seem worried."

"Sorry, I'm not trying to be a downer," he said and pulled Cathy tightly into his chest. She felt immediately comforted by his embrace. "Chris just worries me, and our other friends don't know how bad into stuff he's gotten, so it's a lot of weight to carry around sometimes. That's all."

"Do Marc, Jordan, and Taylor know?"

"I don't think Marc knows. If he did, he would have laid into Luke for selling drugs to Chris. I have no idea about Jordan or Taylor.

Jordan's in Indiana, and Taylor hasn't come home much since his injury."

"That stinks he got hurt. I hope he's able to play in the fall."

"Last I heard, he's recovering from his second surgery. I haven't seen him since Christmas break. I never thought I'd say this, but Chris is actually more of a mess without Taylor or Jordan around," Jason said. "That is incredibly surprising."

"Considering how they party? Yeah, it is."

Jason scowled. "I hope Lisa doesn't drink that drink."

"Should we go check on them?"

"No. They might be having a 'serious convo,'" Jason replied. "Chris wants to 'talk things out with her' and get her to understand that he wasn't 'choosing Jon over her' last summer."

"Well, we need to do *something*," Cathy stated restlessly. "Can we at least order pizza?"

Jason nodded. "Yeah, and let's find a movie to watch on Netflix. I think they'll be upstairs for a while." Something about the look in Jason's eye told Cathy that the drink being offered to Lisa was not as harmless as it sounded.

Chapter 11

Lisa, who was standing in the middle of Chris's bedroom, looked up at him hesitantly. "What will it do to me?" she asked and looked back down at the cup in her hand.

"It will take away all your pain and make you feel really good," Chris replied.

"You've done this before?"

Chris nodded.

"And nothing bad happened to you?"

"I didn't feel very well the next day," Chris admitted, "but otherwise, I was fine."

"How long does it last?"

"Usually about four hours."

Lisa glanced at the clock on Chris's nightstand. "Well it's six o'clock, and Cathy's mom is picking us up at ten-thirty. What if it lasts longer? Will she be able to tell that something is wrong with me?"

"You should be okay by then, but maybe you should only drink half the drink," Chris reasoned. "You can't go to Cathy's house with dilated pupils."

Lisa's heart pounded. "It will mess up my eyes?"

Chris nodded. "Yeah, but they'll go right back down to their normal size afterwards."

She gazed at him skeptically. "Why do you want me to take this with you?"

"Because I miss you," Chris replied immediately, "and I know you're hurting. I've wanted to be there for you all along, but I didn't have the opportunity. I figured the least I could do was cheer you up for a few hours."

Lisa dropped her eyes to the floor. "I'm sorry that I pushed you away."

"People grieve in weird ways," Chris said. "I'm not going to hold anything against you. I'm just glad you're here right now."

When Lisa looked up at him, the sincerity in his eyes melted her heart. "I'm glad I'm here too," she admitted and again looked at the cup in her hand. "What if I just drink a few sips of this to see how it makes me feel?"

"You can drink however much you want. It usually takes about a half hour to kick in. I diluted the powder pretty well in your cup. I think you'd be safe to drink half of it, but if you want to start slower than that, I get it."

"How much are you going to drink?" she asked and nodded toward his cup.

"I put half of a capsule in my cup and a quarter of one in yours," Chris replied. "I'll be fine drinking all of this. It will wear off before my parents get home."

"So, if I drink half of my cup, I will be taking a quarter of what you're going to take?"

Chris nodded.

"That doesn't sound too bad," Lisa murmured and brought the drink to her lips. It looked and smelled like normal soda. "So, I guess, cheers?"

Chris smiled. "Cheers," he said and clinked his cup with hers.

"Did Jay drink some of this?" Lisa asked Chris after putting her cup down on his bureau.

Chris shook his head. "He's afraid Luke will find out."

"Luke gives him weed and pills all the time," Lisa stated matter-of-factly.

"I know, but Jay sees it differently. He likes weed and mushrooms because they're 'natural,' and the pills are really just for Cathy."

"So, he told you about Cathy?"

Chris nodded. "He just did now. He said Luke gave her some benzos to take as needed and that in case she had taken any today, she shouldn't drink any of this."

"Smart," Lisa commented. Her stomach was fluttering, partially because she was excited to be alone with Chris and partially because she was anxious about the drink kicking in. "How will I know when I'm 'rolling?'"

"Oh, you'll know," Chris stated assuredly.

Chapter 12

Cathy and Jason were lying together on Chris's couch, "watching" *Captain America* when the pizza delivery guy arrived. Chris and Lisa were yet to come downstairs, so Cathy and Jason had been making the most of their alone time.

"You should go get the door," Cathy whispered into Jason's ear as he kissed her neck.

"I want you so badly," Jason said quietly.

"Go get the door," Cathy repeated and nudged him playfully.

As Jason climbed off her, Cathy began straightening out the wrinkles on her shirt. She was thankful for the interruption. Restraining herself from letting Jason into her pants was getting more and more challenging. His touch was the greatest feeling of pleasure she knew, and she wanted to experience more of him. However, her head was telling her, over and over again, all the reasons why it was a horrible idea.

When they started dating, Cathy told Jason she planned to wait until marriage to have sex. He replied, saying she could set their pace. She had never imagined that, less than a year later, she would already be entertaining thoughts of losing her virginity to him. At fourteen years old, she was overwhelmed by the thought of having to keep her impulses at bay until marriage.

A moment later, Jason came back into the room, carrying two plates of pizza. He quickly set them down on the table before hopping right back on top of Cathy. First, he kissed her lips, and then he moved onto her neck.

"Stop," Cathy said in such a faint voice that she wasn't sure it had been audible over her pounding heartbeat.

Jason paused. "Stop kissing you?" he questioned her in a perplexed manner.

"Yes," she said flatly.

Jason immediately sat up straight and looked at her with a concerned expression. "Did I do something wrong?"

Cathy shook her head. "No. I'm just… over stimulated… that's all." She smiled at him, hoping that he would not take offense.

"I guess that's a compliment," he said facetiously. "Good thing I know you're an INFJ. That inferior extraverted sensing function of yours really has a mind of its own, huh?"

Cathy laughed. "Leave it to you to psychoanalyze my hormones."

Jason smiled. "Let's eat."

Lisa and Chris came downstairs a few moments later as Cathy and Jason were eating and re-watching the beginning of *Captain America*. "What have you guys been up to?" Jason asked without turning to look at either Lisa or Chris.

"We just caught up a bit," Chris replied and sat down with Lisa on the loveseat.

Cathy looked over at Lisa, trying to decide if she looked extra energized or not. She looked happy to be beside Chris but otherwise completely normal.

"Do you guys want some pizza? There's more in the kitchen," Jason asked, finally turning away from the movie to face his friends.

"Um, no. I'm not really hungry," Lisa replied.

"Yeah, same. I'm good," Chris said.

Cathy watched Jason warily observe Chris. She assumed he was trying to figure out if he had drunk the spiked drink. At the moment, nothing about Chris or Lisa's behavior was startling.

"Do you guys want us to restart the movie?" Jason asked. "Or do you want to watch something else?"

Chris turned to Lisa for a response. She just smiled and shrugged.

"O-kay, then *Captain America* it is," Jason said and let out a sigh. He sounded more frustrated than usual, and Cathy wondered if he thought they had drunk the drink.

"Do you want to lie down across my lap?" Chris asked Lisa.

Cathy turned towards them, a little startled by Chris's frankness. After all, they hadn't hooked back up yet, right?

Lisa paused for a second and eyed him suspiciously before grabbing a pillow and placing it on his lap. "Yes!" she exclaimed.

"Can we lie down on the couch or are you still 'over stimulated?'" Jason whispered to Cathy with a short laugh.

Cathy giggled. "We can lie down," she said and moved aside so Jason could slide behind her. He wrapped his arm around her, and they settled in to watch the movie.

About fifteen minutes later, Lisa abruptly jumped up from the loveseat. She looked at Chris and said, "Oh my gosh!" Then she ran into the nearby bathroom, which could be seen from the living room.

Cathy, startled by Lisa's sudden outburst, sat up straight. She peered across the room to see into the bathroom. Lisa was standing in front of the mirror, staring at her reflection. "Look at my eyes!" she exclaimed.

Chris began laughing.

"@#$%," Jason muttered beneath his breath.

Cathy turned to Jason, expecting an explanation. However, he looked speechless. He was gazing across the room at Lisa and Chris.

"How do you feel?" Chris asked Lisa.

"Oh my gosh. I think I need to sit down. Wow. Yeah. Wow," Lisa replied.

Chris wrapped his arm around her and led her back into the living room. "Just lie down on me," he said.

"An energy drink, Jay?" Cathy questioned him quietly.

Jason let out a heavy sigh. "Yeah. The energy part will come. Just wait."

Lisa let out a soft moan as she laid her head on the pillow on Chris's lap. "I think I just need to take a nap."

Chris looked perfectly content and completely unalarmed while he sat and rubbed her arm.

"What's wrong, Lisa?" Cathy asked loudly.

"Nothing," Lisa replied and then smiled widely without opening her eyes. "I just feel too good to open my eyes."

Cathy glared at Chris. "What did you put in her drink?"

Chris looked confused. "You didn't tell her?" he questioned Jason.

"Yeah, I told her," Jason replied.

"No, you didn't," Cathy protested. "You said it was a drink spiked with something from your brother that gives people energy. Lisa is falling asleep right now."

"What he said is true," Chris stated. "This is just how it usually starts off. She'll come out of it and have a bunch of energy."

"What is 'it?'" Cathy asked, looking back and forth from Chris to Jason.

"Molly," Chris replied matter-of-factly.

Cathy widened her eyes and dropped her jaw before turning to her boyfriend. "You called *ecstasy* an energy drink?!" she cried in dismay.

Jason sighed. "I gave you the definition instead of the term because I didn't want you to freak out over nothing in case they didn't take it. Chris split up a capsule into a couple drinks."

Cathy could understand why Jason had not wanted to worry her, as well as why he would try to save her from having a panic attack, but she would have appreciated more of a warning. She knew Chris had started dabbling with harder drugs than weed, but she had no idea he had already gotten into club drugs.

"Cathy, I just want her to feel happy tonight," Chris said. "She's been in a tremendous amount of pain since last summer, every day."

60

Cathy looked down at Lisa on Chris's lap and saw that she was still smiling.

"You guys are talking like I can't hear you, but I can," Lisa said a few seconds later.

"Why do you seem fine?" Cathy questioned Chris.

"She doesn't weigh much, so it hit her pretty fast. I'll be there soon enough," Chris replied.

Jason put his hand on Cathy's shoulder and looked into her eyes. "If you're uncomfortable, we can leave," he said.

"No! I'm not leaving my best friend like this!" Cathy exclaimed. "How long is this going to last? She can't be like that when my mom gets here."

"She only drank half of her drink, which was half the strength of mine," Chris said, "so she should be fine by ten-thirty."

Suddenly, Lisa sat up straight and glanced at Cathy. Her green eyes looked black because her pupils were so dilated. "We should go do something!" she said brightly.

This must be the energy part.

"Do you guys want to see the cheerleading dance I made up this week?" Lisa asked and jumped off the couch. Without waiting for a response, she lunged into an eight-count dance routine in the middle of the living room.

Cathy didn't know what to say. She just stared at her best friend in awe, feeling a bundle of mixed emotions. It was great to see Lisa smile again—her countenance was definitely the brightest Cathy had seen since her father died—but Cathy was stunned that she was friends with people who had just taken molly. She knew Chris had meant well. Cathy believed he genuinely wanted Lisa to feel some relief from her depression. However, this only proved he was a bad influence on her, and regardless of how great the night turned out to be, it would likely send Lisa running into Jeff's arms.

"I love it!" Chris cried. "Do you want to dance more? I can put on music."

"Yeah. How are you feeling?" Lisa asked, smiling brightly.

"I'm starting to feel pretty good," Chris replied. "Do you want to go upstairs so Cathy and Jay can finish watching their movie?"

Lisa turned toward Cathy and Jason and then turned back to Chris. "Sure!"

As Chris and Lisa hustled upstairs, Jason turned to Cathy and said, "Don't worry about him taking advantage of her while she's like this. Guys usually can't get it up when they're rolling."

Cathy widened her eyes. "Jay, I know Chris. I know he would never take advantage of her. I'm more worried about her taking advantage of him."

Jason looked surprised. "You're not mad at him?"

"No. I get where he's coming from and why he wants to cheer up Lisa. I don't agree with the method, but that was ultimately Lisa's decision, not his," Cathy replied. "I just know she's going to break his heart again if they hook back up."

"Well, MDMA makes people really expressive. Maybe they'll talk out all of their issues and get back together. Who knows?"

"Mr. Psychology, you should know that—unlike, you, me, or Chris—Lisa leads with her head, not her heart," Cathy commented.

"You think she'd be dumb to go back out with Chris?" Jason asked.

"No. That's not what I'm saying. I'm saying, she's already made up her mind. She wants someone stable."

"Well, that's not Chris."

"Right. So, he is trying to do this nice thing for her, and they are probably going to have a great night together, and then she's just going to leave him high and dry."

"Well, he made his bed. He'll have to lie in it. I don't feel bad for him at all. I told him not to offer her molly."

"When did he start doing molly?"

Jason sighed. "I don't know. When did he start doing anything? I think he's just trying whatever Luke throws his way."

"Where does your brother get all this stuff?"

"He won't tell me."

"That's so weird. He became a drug dealer before I even knew he drank alcohol."

"Yeah. Luke made a rash decision, and I'm pretty sure he's testing out the drugs himself. Matt doesn't know. Matt would kill him. He'd freak out and tell our parents. I think the only people who know are his customers."

"Ugh, that sounds so awful. That means we are his customers."

"You've never bought anything from him," Jason reminded her. "You're not a customer, Cathy. He loves you like a sister and is trying to cheer you up; that's all. We remember what you were like before you and Chantal had your falling out. We both just want you to find peace again. I can't imagine what it is like to have a twin in general, let alone be so close and then lose that relationship."

"I'm shocked she hasn't tried to mend things with me yet," Cathy admitted. "All she does is push me away when I try to talk to her about it. It's not very Christian of her."

"No, it's not," Jason agreed and pulled Cathy in for a hug.

"And she thinks she's this super faithful Christian because she goes to youth group, church, and Bible study every week, but she isn't living out her faith. The Bible says to go and talk to someone if you have something against them."

"It also says to forgive people, and she certainly is not forgiving you," Jason said, "for whatever she thinks you did to her."

"I miss her so much," Cathy admitted.

"Everyone misses her, but I still think we did the right thing by not telling her about your theory. Even though Jon is back in 'straightedge' mode, he's still an emotional bomb waiting to explode. She deserves better than that."

"I've hinted at things. Like, I've told her that I think she should hear Alyssa's side of the story and that Jon is claiming she broke up with him," Cathy admitted. "I want her to figure it out on her own because it kills me every day that I'm keeping it from her."

"Do you think that is what's causing your anxiety and depression?"

Cathy sighed. "The depression is definitely from losing my relationship with her. The anxiety, I can't explain. It makes me want to retreat from everyone and everything, which makes no sense because I love people. I'm so happy to finally have a great group of friends. I trust everyone, so I don't understand what brings on the attacks."

"Maybe we should talk to your mom about it," Jason suggested. "Maybe it runs in your family, and you can just go on medication for it."

"No, I don't want to do that. Anxiety meds are addictive, and I don't want to be forced to take something like that every day. If my parents knew how I felt, they would worry too much about me and make me take the medicine as prescribed. I don't want to become an emotional zombie. I think I'll feel better once Chantal makes up with me."

"I think you will too, but how long is she going to take? I mean, she's got to be in love with Andy by now. At this point, she should be glad that Jon 'dumped' her."

Cathy shrugged. "Lisa told me that no one ever gets over their first love, so maybe Chantal still loves Jon after all."

"Well, he certainly still loves her," Jason stated. "Alyssa knows it too, so I don't get why she's dating him."

"It's exactly what Chris told us. They're grieving the loss of Chantal together. That makes perfect sense."

Jason nodded. "I bet Chantal has no idea how much she hurt everyone."

"Probably not. She knows I left Jon an angry message on the day they broke up. She knows Jon is telling people that she broke up with him. I don't understand why she can't put two and two together on her own. She's not stupid."

"She's an ENFP, right?"

Cathy nodded.

"So, basically, she is being blinded by her inferior introverted-sensing function and hibernating in her comfort zone, which consists of only Andy and your parents."

"When you look at the way the human brain works, it all makes perfect sense. However, Chantal isn't knowledgeable about the subject."

"I'm so glad you find psychology interesting," Jason said. "Chris's eyes would glaze over if I tried to talk about this stuff with him."

"What do you think they're doing upstairs?"

"Being idiots," Jason replied. "Chris is definitely rolling by now."

Chapter 13

"I love this song!" Lisa exclaimed as *Living on a Prayer* blared through Chris's Bluetooth speaker. She was lying against Chris on top of his bed. They had been singing song after song at the top of their lungs for the last fifteen minutes. Chris had found a Pandora station that played all the classic rock Lisa used to listen to with her dad. "Listening to all of these songs reminds me of my dad, but it doesn't make sad. It makes me happy. I feel like we are paying homage to him."

"Good," Chris said and rubbed her shoulders. His touch sent waves of pleasure through her body. When his hands moved to her neck, the pleasurable feelings intensified.

"I feel like my whole body is orgasming right now," Lisa admitted.

"I do too," Chris said. "I'm so glad you're here. Do you know it's been six months since you last came over my house?"

"I don't know what I was thinking," Lisa said. "I have never had anything but fun here. You have always done everything in your power to please me. I was in too much pain to see that you were just being a good friend to Jon by refusing to spend time with Andy. I felt like you chose his feelings over mine, so I pushed you away, but I was wrong. You were just being a loyal friend. I put my friendship with Andy before your need for peace."

"Wow," Chris said and kissed Lisa's shoulder. "I'm so glad you can see it that way."

"That just felt so good. Can you keep doing that?"

"You want me to kiss you?" Chris asked her hesitantly.

Lisa wanted him to kiss her more than anything. She had never felt happier to be in anyone's arms. It was the first time she had been in his bed that she didn't want to do anything overly sexual; she just wanted to make out and cuddle. She turned herself around so that she was facing Chris and straddling his body. "I want to kiss *you*," she said and gently kissed his forehead, then his nose, then his lips, and then his cheek.

"I'm so glad you came here tonight," Chris said as Lisa threw her arms around him in an embrace. "I've missed you."

"I've felt so sad since my dad died, but I didn't realize part of the emptiness I've been feeling could also be from not being with you," Lisa admitted. "We were together for almost a year. That's a long time for people our age."

"It is," Chris agreed. "Turn around. I'll rub your back."

Lisa widened her eyes with excitement. "That would be amazing."

"Wow. You're soaked in sweat," Chris commented as he touched the back of her neck.

"I know. Can I take off my shirt? Would that be weird? I have a sports bra on underneath."

Chris laughed. "You can do whatever you want."

Lisa immediately pulled her shirt over her head and tossed it across the room. She closed her eyes and enjoyed the pleasurable waves circulating throughout her body. As Chris rubbed her back, she realized she had never felt so happy in her life. "I think this is the best night of my life, and what you are doing feels amazing."

"I'm glad," Chris said. "I've wanted to see a smile on your face for so long now."

"I made you really sad, huh?" Lisa asked.

"Yup," Chris replied, moving from her back to rub her shoulders.

"Is that why you started trying different drugs? Were you trying to get rid of the sadness?"

"I've definitely been trying to get rid of the sadness, but that sadness didn't start with you. It started a long time ago," Chris admitted. "Losing you made it worse, but at the same time, I was able to appreciate the fact that I had even had you."

67

"I think you are the nicest guy I've ever met," Lisa stated honestly. "All you ever want is for other people to have fun and be happy. I've never seen you be mean to anyone. You don't tease people like Jay or yell at them like Jon. You're much more outgoing than Bryan. You're humbler than Andy. You're friendlier than Jeff. You're not sarcastic like Bobby. You're not overly serious like my brothers. You're just... perfect."

"Thanks, Lis," Chris said and kissed the side of her neck. "I think you're perfect, too."

"If everyone took molly, there would be no war," Lisa concluded. "Seriously. People would be too filled with love to hate each other. Why don't more people do this?"

Chris laughed. "Well, it used to be used for marriage counseling to help couples reconnect and talk out their issues. It was also used to treat soldiers with PTSD. On the streets, I think it's getting popular. People can take whatever size dose they want, so I think more people will do it once they know about it."

"It's not addictive, right?"

"No. It's not like coke or painkillers. Our bodies don't become dependent on it, but you can't do it too much or it will cause depression. All the serotonin raining down your spinal cord right now will be depleted afterwards, and until your brain makes more, you'll feel hungover. That's an oversimplified explanation, but basically it's not something people could do every day without feeling incredibly sick."

"Did Luke tell you that?"

"No. I read about it online. I always read up on things before I try them."

"That's smart," Lisa said. "I probably should have done that. What other drugs have you tried?"

"Weed, mushrooms, ecstasy, mescaline, acid, Adderall, Xanax, Klonopin, and Vicodin, but this one is, by far, the best," Chris replied without any hesitation.

"Wow. You've tried a lot of stuff since we broke up."

"Yeah. I've been a bit bored. I'm just happy you agreed to take this with me. Rolling is no fun by yourself. All you want to do is connect with people, so when you're alone on molly or E, you feel like you're going to go crazy."

"I would not want to be alone right now," Lisa concluded.

"Here. Drink some water," Chris said and reached for a bottle on his nightstand. "You'll get dehydrated if you don't. Drink at least half the bottle."

Lisa was so thirsty, she drank three quarters of the bottle before setting it down on the nightstand. "I want to find more fun music and jump up and down on your huge bed!" she cried before hopping off the bed and running over to Chris's computer.

"Luke said that house music makes you roll even harder. He said the beat makes you 'feel' the music."

"So, Luke does this stuff, too?"

"Luke loves this stuff."

"Jason doesn't know."

"That's for Luke to tell him, not me. I can't even get Jay to drink anymore. I wasn't surprised when he wouldn't try this."

"He loves Cathy too much to drink with you," Lisa said as she perused Chris's list of Pandora stations for anything that looked like it might play house music. She settled for a station that was simply called "Techno."

"This music is so weird, but it actually does make you feel better," Chris said. "Turn it up a little."

Lisa turned up the volume before running back to the bed and jumping on it. She stood up, wearing only her jeans and sports bra, and began bouncing up and down as though she were on a trampoline. "This is really fun!" she cried. Chris was right; the music did make her feel even better.

Chris, who had remained lying down, simply laughed at her.

A few seconds later, Lisa heard a knock at the door.

"Come in!" Chris called.

"Hi!" Lisa greeted Cathy and Jason as they swung Chris's door open.

Cathy widened her eyes and stared at Lisa, as though she were at a loss for words.

"This bed is so good for practicing cheerleading jumps," Lisa said before doing a pike jump. She took a deep breath before speaking. "The ceiling in this room is so high."

"So, that's the noise we heard," Jason said. "We heard a bunch of bangs and wanted to make sure you guys were all right."

"We're great!" Lisa exclaimed and extended her legs into a right hurdler.

"How long does this stuff usually last, Chris?" Cathy asked.

"A few hours," Chris replied.

"My mom will be here in an hour," Cathy said nervously.

"I'm fine, Cathy," Lisa assured her, sensing the concern in Cathy's voice. "I'm getting out all my energy now. I just might make you cuddle with me when we get back to your house."

Jason and Chris looked amused, but Cathy looked horrified.

"Why do you look so shocked? We're best friends. Best friends can hug each other," Lisa stated matter-of-factly.

Cathy let out a short laugh. "I think we might have to come up with a plan B. Your eyes are still black instead of green. My mom is going to know you're on something. Then she'll tell Chris's parents, and this whole thing will blow up in our faces. She'll probably make me take a drug test, and then she'll find out that I smoked weed this month. If your eyes aren't back to normal in forty-five minutes, I'm going to tell my mom you're finding your own ride home because you want to stay out later."

"Okay!" Lisa exclaimed and smiled. "You should really try this, Cathy. It will cheer you up in no time. You won't miss Chantal at all. I'm so glad we're friends."

"I'm glad too," Cathy said, eyeing Lisa warily.

70

"Let's go back downstairs," Jason suggested and tugged on Cathy's arm.

"Bye!" Lisa called as they left Chris's room. She jumped down onto the bed and crawled next to Chris. "Do you want me to give you a back rub?"

Chris widened his eyes. "Yes!" he cried.

"Take off your shirt and roll over," Lisa said excitedly. "I'll sit on your butt!"

Chris laughed and pulled off his shirt. The sight of his muscular torso spread pleasurable vibes throughout Lisa's body. "You look so good," she said, unable to keep her thoughts to herself. "I miss touching those muscles."

Chris rolled over on his stomach. "You can touch them anytime."

"I don't want to leave in an hour," Lisa said as she began running her hands up and down Chris's spine.

"So, don't."

"What will your parents say when they come home and I'm still here?"

"They won't even check on me. If they knock on the door, you can hide in my closet."

"If I stay, I could drink the other half of my drink," Lisa reasoned.

"It's right on the desk."

"If I drink it now, my pupils definitely won't be back to normal when Cathy comes to check on me, so I'll have to stay here."

"Go drink it," Chris said. "Just stir it up before you do."

Lisa pressed her body up against Chris's and rubbed her hands down the sides of his torso. She kissed the back of his head before saying, "Okay!" and then she jumped off the bed.

71

Chapter 14

Lisa finally fell asleep around 7:00 a.m. At 9:47 a.m., she shot her green eyes open and peered at the clock on Chris's nightstand. His arms were tightly around her, and she was happy to still be enjoying his embrace in sobriety. However, her whole body felt weird. There was a vibe running through it that was unfamiliar to her. She needed water; there was no question about that. "Chris," she said quietly and rolled over to face him, "wake up."

Chris opened his blue eyes. "I wasn't really asleep," he admitted and smiled at her.

"How are you going to sneak me past your parents?" she asked.

"Can't you just stay in bed with me all day?" Chris joked.

Lisa laughed and brushed her hand against Chris's face. "Last night was the most fun I've ever had. Thank you for finding a way to lift my spirits for a few hours."

Chris laughed. "For a few hours?!"

Lisa rolled her eyes. "Okay, for, like, ten hours."

"Are your spirits down already?" he asked and ran his hand through her long brown hair.

"They're better than they've been. It helps that I'm still here with you."

"I'm so glad you stayed over. Cathy wouldn't have been able to handle all your dancing, talking, or cuddling last night," Chris said facetiously.

"She's probably pretty mad at me. I don't think she ever expected me to do something like that."

"Cathy's awesome. She won't stay mad at you. Jay's mad at me, but he'll get over it, too. Neither one of them can hold a grudge."

"Ouch!" Lisa exclaimed, suddenly wincing in pain.

"What?!"

"Charlie horse," she said between gasps.

"Oh, you need some water, magnesium, and a banana," Chris said. "Hang here. I'll go grab some stuff from the kitchen. That'll give me a better idea of what my family is up to and how I can sneak you out of here."

"Thanks," Lisa said and tried to straighten out her leg to make the cramp stop. She had never felt so dehydrated in her life.

A few moments later, Chris returned with a couple bottles of water and bananas, as promised. He placed them down on the nightstand and then grabbed a bottle of magnesium off his bureau. "I have to take magnesium every day or I get terrible cramps in my calves and feet," he said and handed Lisa two tablets.

"That's because you work out, every day," Lisa reasoned before washing the tablets down with water. "Can I eat this banana in your bed?"

"What do you want to do with a banana in my bed?!" Chris laughed.

Lisa started laughing hysterically and playfully slapped him in the chest.

"You walked into that one," he said as he hopped back into bed and let out a short laugh.

"Were your parents downstairs?"

"Uh-huh."

"Any idea how I'm going to get by them?"

"Nope."

"Hmmm… well I should call my brother and tell him I'm here. Otherwise, he might call Cathy's looking for me."

"Here," Chris said and passed Lisa his cordless phone. "Hopefully my parents will go out soon, and then they'll just assume you came over while they were gone."

"You want me to spend the day here?" Lisa asked, sounding more surprised than she had meant to.

"If you can," Chris replied. "We have a lot of lost time to make up for."

Lisa's heart fluttered. She loved the idea of spending the day with Chris, because after the previous night she felt closer with him than she ever had. They had only cuddled and kissed, yet she had felt more connected to him than the nights when she had ended up completely naked. Spending the night with him made her realize how much she actually missed him. There was something extremely genuine and kind about Chris that she found attractive. Although she had been contemplating dating Jeff, she realized she needed to sort out her feelings for Chris before she could even think about committing to someone else.

Lisa picked up the phone to call her brother. "Hey, JC," she said after he answered. "I'm going to spend the day at Chris's house."

"Are you guys back together?" JC asked.

"We're trying to figure things out. Can you pick me up here later?"

"Yeah, I can pick you up after work."

"You're working today? But it's Sunday."

"There's just too much to do," JC replied. "It's a good thing, though. Call me around five, and I'll let you know what time I'll be by."

"Okay. Thanks," Lisa said and hung up the phone.

"He's working right now?" Chris asked.

Lisa nodded. "Yeah. He's acting as a paralegal at my dad's office, but the place is in disarray without my dad. The other attorneys on staff had to split up his cases. JC's also in the process of reapplying to law school. He wants to start taking classes part-time as soon as possible."

"Sounds like he has a lot on his plate."

"He does, but he can handle it. He's in a weird position though. He, Joe, and I are the 'owners' of the firm, but none of us are lawyers yet. So, he wants to be in the office all the time to make sure things are running smoothly, but he doesn't have the legal background he needs to understand the way everything works."

"That sounds really stressful," Chris commented. "Is Joe going to work there after he graduates from BU?"

Lisa shook her head. "He's planning to go straight to law school while JC puts his business degree to use and holds down the fort. As long as one of my brothers passes the bar exam in the next few years, we should be okay. Thankfully, the lawyers who work for us worked for my dad for years. They're helping my brother a lot, and he's making sure they're all generously compensated."

"You said none of you are lawyers 'yet.' Does that mean you want to become a lawyer, too?" Chris asked with a sparkle in his blue eyes.

"I think so," Lisa replied.

"You'd be a good lawyer. You're good at getting away with things," Chris teased her.

Lisa laughed. "I've heard that my entire life."

"You told your brother that we are trying to work things out. Is that true?" Chris asked and searched her eyes.

"If you want it to be," Lisa replied, hoping he had meant everything he'd said the previous night.

Chris rolled over so that he was hovering above her in a push-up position. His bare abdomen was brushing up against hers, and she hoped he would start touching her the way he used to when they had been a couple. Before beginning to kiss her, he lowered his chest so that it was nearly flat against her sports bra. First, he kissed her lips, then behind her ear, then down her neck. It wasn't long before he was moving down her abdomen and kissing it every inch of the way. The tender way he touched her made her feel cherished, and she could not understand why she had shut someone so caring out of her life.

"Do I have boyfriend permission?" Chris asked and tugged playfully on the waist of her jeans.

Lisa looked him in the eye and nodded.

Chris smiled widely and then unbuttoned her pants. She was so thin that he was able to slip them off her without even undoing the zipper. When he laid back on top of her, she touched the waistline of his boxers.

He looked up at her in surprise.

"Do I have girlfriend permission?" she asked.

Chris's eyes widened, and Lisa could tell he was shocked. Although Chris had seen her naked a few times, she had never seen him nude. "Really?" he questioned her. His voice came out as a mere whisper.

Lisa swallowed the lump in her throat and then nodded. Chris leaned in to kiss her forehead while she pulled his boxer shorts down to his legs.

"Pull down my underwear and lie naked on top of me," she whispered into his ear.

Again, Chris appeared startled. "Are you sure?" he asked and eyed her warily.

Lisa nodded. "I just want to feel your body up against mine," she replied.

Chris smiled before disappearing under the covers and removing her underwear. When he came back up, he looked nervous.

Lisa ran her hand through his hair. "Just lie down on top of me and hug me tightly," she directed.

"Lis, I've never been completely naked with a girl before," Chris admitted. "I don't want anything to happen by mistake that we're not ready for. I mean, should I put a condom on just in case it rubs up against you?"

Lisa stared into his eyes in an endearing way. "You are the sweetest guy I know," she said. "I trust you to not let that happen."

"Okay," Chris said and let out a heavy breath. He wrapped his arms around her and pulled her body into a tight embrace.

Chapter 15

"You did what?!" Cathy cried into her telephone later that evening.

"I got back together with Chris," Lisa repeated.

Cathy stared blankly across her bedroom in disbelief. She had too many different thoughts going through her mind to reply with a comprehensible sentence.

"He really loves me, and I caused him a tremendous amount of pain when I broke up with him. All he wanted was to be there for me," Lisa said. "I wasn't thinking straight when I pushed him away. I can't believe he didn't move on to anyone else in six months. Every girl at his school has a crush on him."

"What about Jeff?" Cathy questioned her. "What about wanting someone stable?"

"I don't owe Jeff anything. I mentioned to him a few times that I wasn't over Chris. He chose to hook up with me, knowing I had feelings for someone else," Lisa replied defensively.

"Well, you must like Jeff if you were considering calling him your boyfriend," Cathy reasoned.

"I do like Jeff. I'm attracted to him, and I feel safe with him. He's a great student-athlete. He's interested in government and politics. We have a lot in common. He also looks like he just stepped out of an Abercrombie ad," Lisa explained, "but he's not Chris."

"I thought you didn't want to be tied to someone with Chris's reputation?"

"That was shallow of me. Plus, I think Chris could turn things around," Lisa replied. "He's been trying so many drugs lately because he was sad about our breakup. Now that we're back together, he'll probably do fewer drugs."

"You think?" Cathy asked, feeling skeptical. "You guys clearly had a lot of fun last night. You don't think he'll expect you to do molly with him again?"

"Last night was the best night of my life," Lisa admitted, "and it helped me understand myself better. For once, I wasn't afraid to let myself 'feel' things. Today was also a great day. In complete sobriety, we were happy together—so happy that we cuddled, completely naked, for hours, and we didn't have sex."

"That took some restraint."

"It wasn't easy, but neither one of us is ready for sex," Lisa stated.

"You're lucky Chris is a virgin. It must make it so much easier to wait," Cathy remarked.

"Is Jay putting pressure on you?"

"No. I just know he's ready and eager, so I feel bad making him wait. I've never let him in my pants, and he doesn't complain, but he tells me he wants me, like, on a daily basis."

"Of course, he wants you," Lisa said, "but he'll want you less after he has you—just like the other girls he slept with—so hang on to your virginity for dear life if you want to keep Jay's interest."

"It's just hard because he's so hot, and I want him too," Cathy admitted.

"Can't you just pray for strength to resist temptation?" Lisa asked. "Isn't that part of your belief system?"

Cathy's stomach dropped. "I don't think God is very happy with me. I'm supposed to flee from temptation. Instead, I keep spending time alone with Jay and bringing the temptation on myself. I'm my own worst enemy."

"Well, if you don't want to end up sleeping with him, then why do you keep doing that?"

Cathy cocked her head to the side in thought. "I don't know. I'm not being very smart, am I? I guess his affection makes me happy, and I've become addicted to it."

"How much have you told your mom?"

Cathy let out a heavy breath. "Just that we kiss and cuddle. She doesn't know he's seen me with my shirt off."

"Does she know he's not a virgin?"

"No!" Cathy exclaimed.

"Well, then she probably trusts you guys. Keep that in mind, and maybe that will help you keep your pants on."

"Right. I don't want to let down my parents or God. I also don't want Jason to lose interest in me. I've heard sex changes everything. I love the way things are now, and I don't want to lose any of that. It's just that in the heat of the moment, my hormones go crazy, and all I can think about is how badly I want to experience him the way other girls have."

"Your mind is tricking you into thinking it will bring you guys closer if you let him inside of you, but that's all it is—a trick. What makes you close is the connection you share and the friendship you have built over the last year. Sex muddles everything. My brothers have explained it to me over and over again. Quite frankly, I like Chris too much to have sex with him."

"You're so lucky that you can just disconnect from your emotions like that," Cathy said.

"I'm not disconnecting from them; I'm just letting my mind rule over them. I'm being smart."

"Smart?" Cathy questioned her. "You were going to stop hanging out with Chris because he was a bad influence on you."

"True," Lisa agreed, "but last night I realized where I had gone wrong and that Chris is a better person than I had been giving him credit for. Molly made my thoughts clearer, so I'm still listening to my mind; I just have a better understanding of the situation now."

"Are you going to do it again?"

"I doubt it," Lisa replied immediately. "Maybe I would do it if we started having problems and needed to have a really honest conversation. It was such a special night for me; I feel like doing it again would take away from that."

"I'm relieved to hear you say that," Cathy admitted. "I was afraid you were going to start experimenting with drugs like Chris."

"He told me he's tried a bunch of stuff. I don't have any desire to trip or mess with addictive things," Lisa said flatly. "I realized last night that Chris isn't a bad influence on me. My decision to try or not to try things is completely my own. I drank that drink because I wanted some relief from the sadness I've felt non-stop since my dad passed away. The experience made me realize I had only deepened my pain by cutting Chris out of my life."

"I can't believe how much your perspective changed in one day," Cathy remarked. "Is molly a mind-expanding drug?"

"I don't know. I don't think I would have come to these conclusions if I hadn't been with Chris. I think it just helps you connect with the people you are with because every positive thought you have flows out of your mouth without reservation."

"What are you going to do if Chris keeps taking drugs? I mean, I know you are fine with weed, but he obviously likes to drink, and you hate alcohol."

"I bet he'd stop drinking for me," Lisa asserted. "I have a legitimate reason for hating alcohol, and Chris is compassionate."

"You were so worried about me taking Xanax and Klonopin. Aren't you worried about Chris? He doesn't even have anxiety; he takes benzos for fun."

"You are such a downer right now!" Lisa complained. "Kagelli, I know there are some things Chris and I have to work through. I don't want a drugged-up boyfriend. I think he'll lay off things now that we're back together."

"Does he still smoke cigarettes?"

"I have no idea. He didn't smoke last night or today, so he's obviously not addicted to them. I've only ever seen him smoke once, and that was well over a year ago."

"Jason's worried about him," Cathy said. "I can see it in his eyes and hear it in his voice. I'm sure there are things he knows about Chris that he hasn't told me. He might reach out to Marc and let him know Chris has been experimenting with stronger drugs than weed."

"Won't Marc lose it on Luke? Aren't they best friends?"

"Marc would kill Luke, which is why Jason is torn. He's worried about his best friend, but he doesn't want to betray his brother."

"That's a tough spot to be in."

"I don't know how Luke's going to keep it a secret from Matt. They have all the same friends."

"That's Luke's problem—not yours," Lisa reminded her.

"Right, but I have a bad habit of taking on other people's problems," Cathy said. "I can't stand to see anyone in turmoil. I always want to fix things for people."

"You do, but look at where it got you with Chantal," Lisa said. "You helped her get out of that awful relationship with Jon, but she resents you for it."

"She resents me for staying friends with Alyssa—not for sticking up for her with Jon."

"Okay, well there's another example. You felt bad for Alyssa, so you became good friends with her. Now your sister won't talk to you."

"What's your point, Lis?"

"You can't take on everyone's problems because you get hurt in the process almost every time," Lisa replied matter-of-factly. "Empathy is an admirable trait, and I love you for it, but you've got to look out for your own interests from time to time."

"Jason looks out for me. That's why he's researching different medications that might help me feel normal again. My depression, I understand; the anxiety, I don't get. I randomly get panic attacks. It happens to me at parties; it happens at church; it happens during assemblies at school; it comes over me like a blanket."

"You have no idea why?"

"No. My heart starts racing, my palms start sweating, and I feel like I can't breathe," Cathy described. "Sometimes, my whole body breaks out into a sweat, and I feel like the walls are closing in on me. I have no idea what brings it on, and I never know when it's going to hit me, so I'm constantly on edge."

"That sounds horrible. That's why you raced out of the assembly we had at school last week without getting a hall pass?"

"Right."

"Cath, that's not normal. You've got to tell your parents."

"They'll make me go see a doctor or go talk to my pastor," Cathy said. "I already feel like an outcast at church because of all the rumors about me and Jay. Now admitting that I am struck by anxiety would make my pastor think it's because I am dating 'the horrible person' all the kids were talking about. I'm sure he's heard about Jason. His daughter, Jessie, is in our grade."

"I don't blame you for not wanting to get further misjudged by your church, but what's wrong with going to see a doctor?" Lisa probed.

"I've read up on the treatment for anxiety, and the side effects of the medications scare me," Cathy admitted. "My parents would make me take every dose. I don't want to become dependent on a substance just to feel normal. Since I started smoking weed, I've had fewer anxiety attacks. I think it mellows me out enough so that my brain doesn't react to whatever the 'trigger' is. I don't want to walk around stoned all the time, though, so I'm glad I have Xanax from Luke. I can stay sober and just take it when I really need it."

"Did this only begin after you started dating Jason?"

Cathy paused in thought. *When did this start?* "I've always had some social anxiety, but it never brought about physical symptoms. The panic attacks didn't come on until after I had been dating Jay for a while... after your dad died... after Chantal and Jon broke up."

"After she stopped hanging out with you?"

"Actually, yeah. She has no idea that I have panic attacks, so they must have started after our falling out."

82

"Maybe it's twin separation or something," Lisa suggested. "You've got to get her to talk to you. Do you want me to talk to Andy about it?"

"About my mental health? No!" Cathy cried.

"No, about you and Chantal. I can ask him why she won't spend any of her time with you," Lisa offered.

"Sure. It can't hurt," Cathy reasoned. "He must know what she thinks of me."

"Do you think you could get a doctor to prescribe you medicinal marijuana?" Lisa asked. "Then you could just eat gummies every day to prevent panic attacks, and you wouldn't have to smoke it. I know you hate smoking it."

"My parents would never go for that," Cathy replied. "It makes no sense to me because marijuana is less addictive than most prescription meds, but they think it's a gateway drug and that it's sinful."

"Why do you think getting drunk is a sin but not getting high?" Lisa asked curiously.

"Because the Bible says not to be drunk, but it doesn't say not to be relaxed. I figure if God made marijuana, He had a reason for it. Like Jay always says, it's natural."

"Yeah, but cocaine and heroin also come from plants," Lisa stated. "Using those would be sinful, right?"

"Yeah, but those impair people's judgement. The Bible says to lead a sober life. It doesn't say drinking is a sin; it says being drunk is a sin."

"Hmmm," Lisa said thoughtfully. "I agree with you about weed versus alcohol. I have my own reasons for hating alcohol, but even if a drunk driver didn't kill my father, I think I would have realized how detrimental it can be to relationships. Jon and Chantal were fine before he started drinking; it brought out the worst in him. Smoking weed, on the other hand, hasn't caused any problems for you and Jay. That's why I agreed to try it. I realized it didn't turn you into a bad person."

83

"Well, I'm glad you don't think I'm a bad person," Cathy said with a short laugh. "I believe it's sinful to take any substance that impairs your reasoning, but taking something to relieve pain or anxiety is fine. A lot of pain meds come from the same plant heroin is made from, and there is definitely a need for those. Problems start when people abuse them."

"I feel better after talking to you about this," Lisa commented. "I was scared when you told me you took Xanax. Now, I get what you're trying to do. I probably scared you when I took molly, huh?"

"Um, *yeah*," Cathy said with emphasis, "but I'm glad you don't want to do it again. I hope you can get Chris to stop drinking and experimenting with things."

"You'd never guess because he always wears a smile on his face, but he's so sad inside," Lisa said. "I think that's why he always tries to make everyone happy. He knows how awful it is to feel sad, so he focuses on cheering up other people."

"Where does his pain come from?"

"He has believed since he was a child that his parents don't love him," Lisa replied. "They've never told him they love him, and they spend half the year in Europe. They don't make a big deal out of his birthday or holidays. Half the time he spends Christmas without them. He thinks they value expensive things over time spent with him and Katie. His whole sense of self-worth is askew because the people who were supposed to teach him what love is have only shown him what love is not. A nanny raised him and Katie, and they were quite attached to her, but his parents fired her once Taylor was old enough to housesit because they didn't want to pay her. That's insane to me. Taylor was a senior in high school at the time. They would rather have their kids watched by a wild teenager than pay a supportive and caring nanny, who had proven herself year after year."

Wow. "I can see why he think his parents don't love him," Cathy remarked. "You would never know he carries that baggage around with him because he's our most fun friend."

84

"He's pretty open about this stuff with me. He said I'm the first person he's ever felt truly loved by. He thought his nanny loved him, but in the back of his mind, he never knew if she was in it just for the money. Either way, his parents cared more about saving money than Chris's or Katie's attachment to the woman who raised them. The worst part is they totally have the money. Their flat in London is worth over a million dollars. No wonder they spend more time there than in Montgomery."

"How did Chris turn out to be such a nice person?" Cathy wondered.

"Pain breeds compassion or anger," Lisa replied matter-of-factly. "He chose compassion."

Chapter 16

As the winter progressed, Cathy continued to battle with anxiety and depression while Chantal continued shunning Cathy and the rest of her friends. Every day, Cathy would pray for her sister's heart to soften. Whenever she would read a devotional or flip through pages in her Bible, she would come across scriptures about the truth being revealed in God's perfect timing. Focusing on that gave her a sense of peace, and she realized that she needed to stop obsessing over their relationship.

Lisa and Chris continued enjoying their rekindled relationship. Chris promised Lisa that he would not drink around her, even at parties. This pleased Lisa, and for that reason, she did not come down hard on him when he took Adderall, painkillers, or Xanax. Keeping him away from alcohol was most important to her. Because neither Lisa, Jon, Alyssa, Cathy, nor Jason drank alcohol, it made it much easier for Chris to abstain from it.

One Saturday in early April, Lisa went to Connecticut with her brothers for their cousin's wedding. It happened to be while Marc was housesitting. Unlike Jordan or Taylor, Marc never threw huge parties, but he did invite his group of friends over for the evening. Chris had not been invited to Lisa's cousin's wedding, so he invited Cathy, Jason, Jon, and Alyssa to his house. When Cathy and Jason arrived, they were surprised to see Chris drinking. He had not touched alcohol, to their knowledge, in almost two months. He seemed to get drunk quite quickly, and Cathy assumed it was because he had lost his tolerance.

That night marked the first time Luke ever offered Cathy and Jason opiates. "If you take one of these, you'll just feel drunk off less beer," he said to them in Chris's upstairs bathroom.

"I don't even drink," Jason stated. "I'm all set."

"You don't have any weed or Xanax?" Cathy asked.

"Sorry, CK. I don't," Luke replied. "If you take one of these and drink a beer, you'll feel relaxed. Trust me."

Cathy's stomach turned. "Drinking is against my morals, and I hate trying things for the first time."

"When you broke your ankle, did your doctor give you anything for the pain?" Luke asked.

"Yeah, Motrin and Tylenol with Codeine," Cathy replied.

"Okay, so, that's basically the same thing as Vicodin," Luke said, "but I'm not trying to talk you into this; I just want you to feel comfortable around all the high school kids here."

"Well… I was fine on Tylenol with Codeine," Cathy stammered and slowly extended her hand to take the Vicodin from Luke. "I'll just wash it down with water instead of alcohol."

About a half hour after Cathy took the pill, her body felt light, and she felt happier than she had in a long time. She could not deny that she liked its effect even more than that of weed or Xanax. However, she had an empty stomach, and the pleasurable feeling throughout her body quickly dissipated as nausea ensued.

"I'm so sorry, babe," Jason said as he knelt down on the floor beside Cathy in Chris's upstairs bathroom. He rubbed her back as she threw up in the toilet.

"I can't go home like this," Cathy said between heaves. "My parents will think I've been drinking. They'll kill me."

"No, they won't. They'll think you have a stomach bug. You're perfectly sober."

Cathy was soaked in sweat, and chills were spreading throughout her body. "I hate this."

"If you call your mom to come get you now—way before your curfew—she will definitely think you are just sick," Jason reasoned. "I can call her if you want."

Cathy nodded and took a deep breath. She wiped sweat off her forehead. "Do that. Tell her that I'm sick to my stomach and need to go home. You're right; it's early, and I haven't had a sip of alcohol. She'll assume I ate something that didn't agree with me, which is technically true."

"Yeah, Vicodin," he said with a short laugh. He pulled his iPhone out of his pocket and called Cathy's house. "Hi, Chantal, is your mom home?" he asked a few seconds later. "Oh, okay. Is your dad home?" Pause. "I'm at Chris's with Cathy, and she needs a ride home. She ate something that isn't agreeing with her, and she just threw up." Pause. "Okay, well, I'll see if one of my parents can come get her. I don't want to bother your parents if they're out."

"I feel bad making your parents come out to get me," Cathy said once Jason ended the call. "I forgot that my mom and dad were going into Boston for dinner with my aunt and uncle."

"I'll run downstairs and ask Matt if he can give you a ride home," Jason said. "You can trust he'll be sober enough to drive."

"Thanks," Cathy said and rested her head against the bathroom wall.

Jason took the ride with Matt to bring Cathy home, and thankfully, she did not throw up in his Lexus SUV. Cathy called her mother's cell phone once she got home and told her that she had gotten a ride home and was going to bed. After eating some toast and drinking some ginger tea, Cathy felt less nauseous, but she still could not wait to crawl into bed.

"How was Chris's?" Chantal asked as Cathy passed by her in the hallway.

"Fine," Cathy replied lifelessly. "Marc is housesitting this time, so it was mainly juniors in high school and my friends."

"Was Jon there?"

Cathy nodded, wondering why her sister cared. She had been happily dating Andy for over six months.

"With Alyssa?"

"Yeah, but why do you care?" Cathy asked. "Aren't you happy with Andy?"

"I love Andy," Chantal retorted defensively. "I just worry about Jon; that's all. He doesn't even come to church anymore."

"Jon's fine," Cathy stated flatly, "and he's not your problem to worry about—he's Alyssa's problem."

"Are they happy together?"

Cathy sighed. "Tal, why do you care?"

Chantal shrugged. "I try not to; I just do. I simultaneously detest and miss them both."

Cathy's heart began to pound in her chest. She hated the sadness she saw in her sister's eyes. It still bothered her every day that she had unintentionally sabotaged Chantal's relationships with both Alyssa and Jon. Although Cathy still believed Andy was better for her sister, she hated that Chantal erroneously believed Alyssa had backstabbed her. "I still think you should try to talk things out with Alyssa."

"I don't get it," Chantal said with aggravation. "You always defend her. You've practically become best friends with the girl who stole my boyfriend. Do you realize how much that hurts me?"

"I've told you a million times that I don't think Alyssa backstabbed you," Cathy stated defensively. "She did not hook up with Jon until you were already dating Andy. She did not steal your boyfriend, and I think you should hear her side of the story."

Chantal let out a heavy breath. "Jon told me he was going to date her, and then he did just that! Why wouldn't I believe she backstabbed me?"

"Alyssa was always a good friend to you, and she has always been a good friend to me. She is not malicious. Jon has a terrible temper! He threw her under the bus in a fit of anger; he was probably mad about the voicemail I left him earlier that day," Cathy reasoned. "I am not going to stop being friends with her just because her boyfriend was a jerk to you. Jason and I both stopped being friendly with Jon because of the way he treated you. I thought that would be enough to prove our loyalty to you, but it wasn't. You cut us both out of your life. You turned

89

your back on Chris, Lisa, Bryan—everyone! You shut all of us out, and you don't seem to care how deeply you've hurt *me!*"

Chantal widened her eyes, clearly surprised by Cathy's rant. Expressing her emotions so blatantly was quite uncharacteristic of Cathy. "You obviously don't realize how much you've hurt me," Chantal retorted. "I know you hated me with Jon; Lisa is happy now that I'm dating Andy; and I'm sure Alyssa is happy to be Jon's girlfriend. I don't believe for a second that their relationship is a consequence of my relationship with Andy. It's also not a coincidence. You all got exactly what you wanted."

Cathy dropped her jaw. "What is *that* supposed to mean? All I have ever wanted is for you to be happy."

Chantal rolled her eyes. "All you've ever wanted is to be popular."

"Woah! Where did that come from?"

"You must be happy dating the most sought-after boy in our grade and being best friends with two of the prettiest girls in Montgomery."

Cathy widened her eyes in awe. "Are you mad at me for having friends?"

"You chose your friendships with them over your relationship with me," Chantal stated. "That has been clear to me since you became friends with Alyssa again. You didn't want to rock the boat, so you stayed friends with someone who betrayed me, and you still hang out with Jon—the boy who broke my heart!"

"I wanted all of us to stay friends! You are the one who distanced yourself from everyone. You chose not to talk things out with Jon or Alyssa. You still see Lisa all the time when you're out with Andy, but you aren't friendly to her. Leslie and Katherine told me you're not even friendly to them! It's like you shut off your ability to connect with people. Everyone I hang out with misses you. In our eyes, you cut us out."

"That's because you all betrayed me, and I can't trust any of you," Chantal said. "Not even you."

Cathy felt her eyes begin to fill up with tears. "You are my twin sister. Don't you feel the void in your life without me? Every day, I am sad because you stopped being my friend. Every day, Jason has to find some way to cheer me up because I am lost without our relationship."

Chantal began to cry. "Then why did you have to befriend Alyssa?"

"She was already my friend," Cathy replied as a stream of tears poured out of her right eye. "I had no idea it would cause this much dissention between us."

"But it was a risk you were willing to take to keep your popular group of friends."

Cathy stared at her sister in wide-eyed disbelief. "You have it so wrong," she said and shook her head sadly. "Once you find it in your heart to forgive Jon, you will find out the truth. Jon told everyone you broke up with him for Andy. Chris and Bryan believe that, but they're not even mad at you because they think Jon was being a jerk to you. Jon forced Chris to stop hanging out with Andy, which ruined his and Lisa's relationship for a while. Either Jon is the biggest liar we know or there was a miscommunication between the two of you. I promise you that Alyssa had nothing to do with your breakup."

"Interesting theory," Chantal commented dryly before pushing past Cathy and storming into her bedroom. Nausea returned to Cathy's stomach, but it had little to do with the Vicodin and everything to do with Chantal.

Chapter 17

Around seven o'clock on Sunday morning, Cathy awoke to the sound of her telephone ringing. Cathy and Chantal shared a line, so she knew it had to be one of their friends calling. Who would call so early on a Sunday was the question. "Hello?" she called groggily into her cordless phone.

"Cathy, you've got to pray for Chris," Jason said in a serious tone.

"What? What's wrong?" she asked while struggling to keep her eyes open.

"Last night, you know how he was drinking? Well, Luke gave him Vicodin, and he took Xanax before we got there."

"Holy crap!" Cathy cried in dismay.

"He got so sick. His breathing was so shallow that I thought he was going to die. Jon and Alyssa had already left when it happened, but Luke and I were still here. Luke had coke, so Marc told Chris to do it to stimulate his body."

"What?! Marc made him do coke?!"

"Marc didn't know he had taken Vicodin or Xanax. He thought Chris was just extremely drunk. Coke sobers people up, so he told Chris to do it."

"That is insane. Is Chris okay?"

"We almost called 9-1-1, but Chris finally came out of it. I have never been so scared in my life. I thought I was going to watch my best friend die. I don't know what Chris was thinking, but he really messed up."

"Why would he mix so many drugs together?" Cathy asked, feeling wide awake and sick to her stomach. "He's so lucky he didn't OD."

"I know! He's finally asleep, but Marc and I haven't been to bed yet. We had to watch him and make sure he kept breathing. We knew the consequences of calling 9-1-1 but also the risk of not calling. Please pray that we made the right decision. I am beside myself right now."

"Of course, I'll pray," Cathy said. "Lisa is going to be so upset. One night without her around and he went off the rails."

"Don't tell her. If he wants to tell her, he will. When he wakes up, Marc is going to have a long talk with him."

"I can't believe that happened. That must have been so scary for you," Cathy said and rubbed her forehead. "Are you going to try to get some sleep?"

"Yeah. I'm going to sleep in Chris's bed so I can easily check on him. He's breathing normally now, and he hasn't thrown up in a few hours, so I don't think he'll choke. Marc's going to come up here and check on him, too. We'll call an ambulance if we need to, but I think he's in the clear."

"I'm so sorry you had such a horrible night. I thought my night was bad because Chantal flipped out on me when I got home, but yours was way worse."

"What's Chantal's problem?"

"She told me she thinks I chose having popular friends over staying loyal to her. She thinks all I want is to be popular and that I betrayed her by being friends with Alyssa. She also said she thinks Lisa, Alyssa, and I all got exactly what we wanted and that Alyssa and Jon's relationship is no coincidence."

"Wow. She really thinks all that? You don't care about popularity; you just wanted her to be treated right," Jason said, sounding dismayed.

"I know. I told her she had it all wrong. I basically told her everything she needs to put the puzzle together, but she blew off my idea. She called it an 'interesting theory.'"

"You are definitely the brighter twin," Jason stated. "It sounds like she thinks you, Lisa, and Alyssa all plotted the breakup together."

"If she thinks that, then she is crazy!" Cathy exclaimed.

"Well, I'm sorry, babe," Jason said downheartedly. "I don't know what her problem is with you, but all you can do is hope she'll come around."

"I wish she would just talk to Jon and find out the truth," Cathy said with frustration. "She is so stubborn."

"Speaking of Jon… don't tell him or Alyssa about what happened to Chris. Marc doesn't want anyone to know. You are the only person I'm telling. Don't tell Lisa; don't tell anyone."

"I won't," Cathy pledged. "I'm sure Chris will end up telling her. She's going to get very upset."

"Hopefully that will wake him up to how ridiculous he's been acting lately," Jason stated. "I'm going to try to sleep for a bit. I'll call you later, okay?"

"Okay."

"Good morning and good night."

"Same. Love you. Bye," Cathy responded and hung up the phone. She could not believe what Jason had just told her. She felt sick to her stomach at the thought of Chris mixing so many different drugs together. *Dear God, please send Chris the help he needs to straighten out his life. He is the nicest person I know, but he's such a mess. Please heal his heart. He's trying to fill a void that I believe only you can fill. Please let this experience wake him up, and please give him the courage to be honest with Lisa. She deserves to know the truth. In Jesus name I pray, Amen.*

Chapter 18

Chris shot his blue eyes open at the sound of his phone ringing. His vision seemed a bit blurry, and his body ached worse than it had after a week of football camp. He glanced at the clock on his nightstand: 1:27 p.m. The ringing drilled through his ears like a jackhammer. After sending the call to voicemail without paying attention to the caller ID, he realized he was still fully clothed from the night before. Jason was sleeping beside him in his bed, and Marc was asleep on his futon.

Thirty seconds later, his phone began to ring again, drawing his attention to the name on the screen: Lisa. He let out a slight moan as he reached for his phone and answered the call. "Hi," he greeted her, surprised by how hoarse his voice sounded.

"@$#%! You sound terrible!" Lisa exclaimed.

"Yeah, I do."

"Did you get my voicemails? I've been trying to get ahold of you since ten o'clock last night."

Chris rubbed his forehead. "Lis, I have no idea. I just woke up in bed with Jay in the clothes I wore yesterday, feeling like I was hit by a truck."

"Did you drink last night?"

"I… I… I think so."

"What do you mean: you 'think' so?" she asked, sounding perturbed.

"Uh, my brain's a little fuzzy right now, and I can't remember anything about last night."

"So, you must have gotten drunk."

"I took Xanax before everyone came over," Chris admitted, "but Xanax has never made me feel as sick as I feel right now. Either I have the flu or the worst hangover of my life."

"Why is Jay in bed with you?"

"I don't know. I seriously just woke up. Marc is sleeping on my futon. They must be exhausted because neither one of them woke up when the phone rang."

"Well, I just got back from Connecticut, and I was hoping to come over."

"I think I might need to go to the hospital."

"What?!"

"My body doesn't feel right. I'm going to wake up Jay and find out what happened last night. I'll call you back in a bit," he said and ended the call. He didn't mean to sound rude, but he was slightly freaked out. After setting his phone down on the nightstand, he nudged Jason hard in the shoulder.

"Ugh, you're awake?" Jason questioned him rhetorically while squinting his blue eyes open.

"What the hell happened last night?" Chris asked frantically. "Why are we in bed together, and why do I feel like I have mono?"

Jason sat up straight. "You don't remember?"

"Remember what?"

"Dude, you almost ended up going to the hospital last night."

"What are you talking about?"

"You almost overdosed."

Chris lowered his eyebrows. "On what?!" he exclaimed.

"On everything," Jason replied.

Chris looked over at Marc, who was still sound asleep. "What happened?"

Jason sighed. "You drank on Xanax. That's why you can't remember anything. Then when Luke showed up, he gave you Vicodin, and you kept drinking."

"I took Xanax and Vicodin while drinking?" Chris asked, widening his eyes in horror.

Jason nodded.

"What the hell was I thinking? I could have died!" Chris cried.

"I think you almost did. When Marc wakes up, you two need to have a *long* talk. I have never been more scared in my life. Oh, you also did a line of coke."

"I've never touched coke!"

"That's not true at all."

"You're saying I mixed alcohol, Xanax, Vicodin, *and* coke?"

Jason nodded. "I'm also saying you almost killed yourself."

"Is this some type of joke?"

"No," Jason stated seriously. "This is definitely not a joke."

"Why would I ever take Vicodin if I was on Xanax?"

"I have no freaking idea. I wasn't here when Luke gave you Vicodin. I left with Matt to drive Cathy home. After we got back, you passed out in the living room, and Luke told me you had taken Vicodin. I knew you had taken Xanax earlier in the night. At that point, I wanted to call an ambulance. Then Marc came rushing into the room. He didn't know about the pills, so he thought you were just drunk. When you came to, he brought you upstairs and told you to do a line of coke to sober up. It stimulated you, but I don't know if it made things better or worse."

"Wait a minute. I passed out in front of everyone? Marc told me to do coke? *Marc*? He doesn't touch drugs. Who had coke?!"

"Luke."

"Marc would never tell me to do coke; none of this makes any sense."

"Oh, look who's awake," Marc suddenly spoke up from across the room. He sat up straight on the futon and glared at Chris.

Chris could feel his face turning bright red.

"I'm going downstairs to cook lunch so you guys can talk," Jason said and jumped out of bed. As Jason hurried out of the room, Chris stared blankly at the wall in front of him, trying to process everything his friend had just said.

"You have a big problem," Marc stated in an extremely serious tone. "Your parents need to know about this. This is beyond typical teenage stuff. You could have overdosed last night. I don't know who you got Xanax from, but Jason told me you took it earlier in the night. I saw you drinking all night long. Mixing benzos with alcohol is beyond dangerous."

Chris stared at Marc like a deer in headlights.

"You need to go to AA with my dad or join Teen Challenge," Marc continued. "You are a mess, and I don't know how to help you. You could have died on my watch. I never could have lived with myself if that had happened. How could you be so irresponsible?"

Chris let out a heavy breath. "I'm wicked stupid. I'm a mess. I'm a horrible person," he ranted, believing every single word he spoke. "I don't know what else to say. I'm sorry I put you through that—you, Jay, and everyone else. I'm out of control, and I clearly have impaired judgement. I think I should go to the hospital to make sure I'm okay."

"I'll bring you, but if there's still alcohol in your blood, then you're going to open a can of worms."

"Let's wait a few more hours just to be safe. I'll say I have flu-like symptoms. They'll check all my levels and give me IV fluids. I have never felt this hungover in my life."

"I need to tell your parents about this. I can't carry this around on my chest."

"Tell them. They won't care."

"Of course, they will."

Chris shook his head. "Tell them everything. Tell them I did coke, drank beer, and mixed Xanax with Vicodin. Tell them what a mess I am and see if they do anything."

"What are you talking about? You took Vicodin?"

"Evidently. That's what Jay just told me."

"When I told you to do coke, I thought you were just drunk. I've seen it sober Taylor up so many times that I thought it would help you. I never would have given it to you if I knew you had Xanax and Vicodin in your system. It is a miracle that you didn't stop breathing last night."

"Why did you have coke?"

"Luke said someone gave it to him to try. I was too freaked out about you to question him."

"Luke does coke now? He's only in tenth grade."

"You're only in eighth grade! Look at what you did last night! You two are both speeding down the highway to hell."

Chris's heart sank. "I don't want to live like this. I don't want to become a drug addict. I want to be a good student and get a football scholarship to college. This isn't the life I want."

"Then you need to make some serious changes because you've let some very dark things take a grip on you."

"Lisa is going to kill me when she hears about this."

"The only people who know you mixed alcohol with drugs are me, Luke, and Jason. None of us want this to get around. We could all get in trouble."

"Jason equals Cathy, and Cathy equals Lisa, so she probably already knows."

"Your girlfriend is not your biggest problem right now. Why the hell did you take Xanax last night? Who is selling pills to you? Pills will ruin your life."

"Just a kid I know," Chris replied and put his head down. "I don't do it a lot; I just wanted to feel relaxed around your friends."

Marc stared at Chris blankly.

"I'm an idiot," Chris added. "Everything you and Jay just said about last night is horrifying."

"You have a serious problem," Marc said. "And I hope to God your parents can find you the help you need."

"What are you going to tell them?"

"That you drank on Xanax and got so sick that I almost called 9-1-1. I'll leave out the other stuff because the first part is horrific enough to get their attention. They won't be home for two more days. Can you stay alive until then?"

Chris hung his head. "I'm sorry. You shouldn't have to deal with this. I made a really bad decision when I drank on Xanax. It made me forget, which is probably why I agreed to take Vicodin later in the night."

"Whoever this person is who is selling you drugs—block their phone number. Cut them out of your life. If you want to get sober, you need to stop hanging out with people who do drugs."

"My friends don't do drugs," Chris said defensively.

"I've seen every one of your close friends high except for Alyssa, whose brother would kill her if she touched a drug," Marc said matter-of-factly. "You are in denial if you think your friends are good influences."

"Okay, so, *some* of my friends have experimented with things, but Jon went completely straightedge after losing Chantal, and Lisa stopped drinking after her father's accident. Actually, Lisa, Jon, Cathy, Jay, and Alyssa all don't drink. Bryan hasn't touched a drug since last year. My friends are not the problem; I'm the problem."

"Your friends are part of the problem, Chris," Marc insisted. "You just can't see it."

"Your best friend does coke!" Chris cried out defensively.

"I just found that out last night, and if he's going to keep doing it, then I'm going to distance myself from him."

"Are you going to tell Matt?"

"About you or Luke?" Marc asked.

"Luke."

Marc sighed. "I don't know. I don't want to get in the middle of them. They're my two best friends."

"I need to call Lisa and explain everything to her. It will be best if she hears it first from me. She's going to be so disappointed," Chris said downheartedly. "I need to take a nap before I can even think about having that conversation."

"Get some sleep," Marc said. "Now that I know you're okay, I'm going to go sleep in your parents' room. Wake me up when you want a ride to the hospital. Just make sure you feel completely sober before we go."

Chris fell back to sleep within a few minutes, but he kept waking up periodically with cold sweats. *There has to be more to life than this,* he thought as he closed his eyes.

Chapter 19

Later that night, Chris sat between Lisa and Marc in the emergency room's waiting area. He had not yet told Lisa the details of the previous evening, and he feared her reaction. She had insisted on going to the hospital with him when he called her after his nap. Chris could tell she was worried about him, and he felt horrible for ruining both her and Marc's Sunday night.

"I'm going to walk to Dunkin' Donuts and get you a Gatorade. Marc, do you want something?" Lisa asked after they had been anxiously waiting hours for Chris's name to be called.

"An iced coffee with almond milk and no sugar, please," Marc replied. "I'll text you if they bring him to a room. Here's some money."

"Don't worry about it," Lisa said and pushed Marc's hand away from her. "I'll just pay with the app. I'll hurry back."

The longer Chris waited to tell Lisa the truth, the guiltier he felt. However, he could not admit to such heinous behavior while sitting inside a packed waiting room. *If I had overdosed last night, I could have died before the ambulance got me here. Lisa's heart would have shattered into pieces. She can't lose her father and her boyfriend in one year—especially not to alcohol-related incidents,* Chris thought as he reflected on how bad the consequences could have been. *What is wrong with me? I have scared and hurt so many people who deserve so much better than this. How did I become so selfish?* In his fourteen years on Earth, Chris had never hated anyone more than himself.

After another half hour, Chris was taken into a room in the ER, where they re-checked his vital signs and drew a few vials of blood. They hooked him up to IV fluids and allowed him to drink the Gatorade Lisa had bought for him. The results of the bloodwork showed no liver or kidney damage. Some of his levels were off due to dehydration, but otherwise his readings were all within normal range.

"Do you spend a lot of time outside?" the doctor asked.

"I play a lot of sports outdoors," Chris replied.

"I'm going to order a tick panel, just to rule out Lyme, Bartonella, Babesia, and a few other infections that can cause the aches and pains you are describing. You have no numbness or tingling anywhere, though, right?"

Chris shook his head.

"Okay. We have your blood on file. I'll order the tests, and if you are positive for any infections, we will call you. Otherwise, I would say this is likely just a virus. Your bloodwork shows no sign of infection, so antibiotics will not help. We'll have you finish the bag of fluids and get your discharge papers ready."

"Thank you," Chris said and shook the doctor's hand.

"That's really good news," Lisa commented after the doctor left the room. "Are the fluids making you feel better?"

Chris nodded, closed his eyes, and rested his head against a pillow. "I'm so sorry you two had to spend your Sunday night here," he said without opening his eyes.

"It's a good thing your parents were able to fax over the consent form so the hospital could treat you. They think you have the flu, so be prepared to tell them the truth when they get back," Marc stated in a serious tone.

"You didn't tell them what happened?" Chris asked and shot his blue eyes open.

Marc shook his head. "I decided it needs to come from you. I'm going to tell Jordan, Taylor, and my dad, though. So, keep in mind that if you don't tell your parents soon, they'll hear it from other people in our family."

"Considering what Taylor's been up to lately, he won't lay into me about this," Chris said. "I think the meds he's on are messing with his head."

"He's definitely depressed," Marc said, "and that alone can change someone's personality, but I think you're right about the pain meds he's taking. My parents told me his GPA has dropped significantly. He's in danger of failing out of the business program."

"What?!" Chris cried. "He's usually on the Dean's List."

"I can't make sense of it," Marc said. "He hardly ever comes home or calls. Something's wrong with him."

"I know I'm the last one who should be asking this, but do you think he's abusing his pills?" Chris asked.

Marc let out a heavy breath. "At this point, anything is possible with him. I'm going to visit him this week and try to figure out where his head's at."

"Good," Chris said and again shut his eyes.

"Will you do me a favor and figure out where *your* head is at?" Lisa spoke up and slapped Chris's arm.

Chris opened his eyes and looked at her sadly. "After we get out of here, can you come back to my house and talk?"

Lisa nodded.

"I just don't want to expose things here," he explained.

"I get it, but I want to know everything," Lisa stated.

Chris sighed. "You will."

After leaving the hospital, he began to agonize over telling Lisa the truth. Nevertheless, the truth was what she deserved. Once they arrived at his house, Chris led Lisa upstairs to his bedroom. He pulled her down beside him on the bed and stared at her for a few seconds before beginning to speak. He took in her beauty and reminded himself of how lucky he was to have had a second chance with her.

"Lis, you're really not going to like what I have to say," Chris began and shook his head. He did not even feel worthy enough to hold her hand. "I took Xanax before the party last night, and I drank on it."

Lisa peered at him expectantly.

"You can't drink on Xanax or you'll black out, which I did. The next thing I remember is waking up to your phone call this afternoon. Evidently, when I was in a drunken blackout, I thought it would be okay to take Vicodin and snort a line of coke."

104

Lisa's green eyes grew wider than Chris had ever seen.

"Marc told me to do coke to sober up because he thought I was just drunk," Chris added. "He didn't know about the pills. I swear I've never touched coke otherwise."

"You mixed all those drugs together?" Lisa questioned him, sounding shocked.

Chris nodded. "My guess is when I took the Vicodin, I forgot about the Xanax. I know how dangerous it is to mix them. The thing is, I also know how deadly it can be to drink on Xanax, but I still did it. That was a conscious choice I made at eight o'clock last night when I poured myself a beer."

"Alcohol ruins everything," Lisa said sadly and looked away from him.

"No. People ruin things; I ruin things," Chris stated and pointed at himself. "I am my own worst enemy, Lisa. I'm messed up. I'm really messed up. Okay? Do you get what I'm saying? I didn't just mess up; I *am* messed up. I could have died last night." He became choked up as he spoke. "I could have shattered your already broken heart into a million pieces."

Lisa looked up at him, and Chris dropped his teary eyes to the floor.

"You deserve so much better than this," he added.

"I thought you stopped drinking for me," Lisa said in a tone that expressed her disappointment.

"I did stop drinking for you, but I should have stopped drinking for me. You weren't around, so I decided it was harmless to have a beer. God knows how many I drank before I decided to take Vicodin. Can't you see how dangerous it is to be in my life?"

"Maybe Jay and Marc are just trying to scare you straight? Maybe they exaggerated? Maybe you weren't really that bad?" Lisa suggested.

"I know you want that to be the truth, but it's not. Jay and Marc stayed up all night long to take care of me."

105

"Maybe they talked, and this is their way of making you realize that you need to tone it down?"

"What are you saying? That they conspired and made everything up?"

Lisa shrugged. "I'm just saying there's a possibility that they might have exaggerated. You might not have taken Vicodin or done coke. You might have just been a mess because you drank on Xanax. That is dangerous enough."

"Marc and Jay would never lie to me," Chris stated assuredly.

"I believe they would if they thought it would save your life," Lisa said. "I wouldn't be mad at them about it either."

"I've never had a hangover worse than this in my life," Chris admitted. "If someone gave me a drug test right now, I'm certain everything would show up."

"Well, I don't have a drug test, but I have an open mind, and I doubt you were the complete mess they made you out to be. If you were that bad, then they would have called 9-1-1."

"Lis, I understand why you want to believe that, but the fact that I can't remember if I did coke or not is a problem in itself," Chris stated matter-of-factly. "You should be able to go to your cousin's wedding without me putting my life in danger. I am not a good boyfriend; I get high every day. I'm not a good son or brother. My grades are slipping, and instead of doing my homework, I come home from practice and get stoned. I make horrible decisions every single day."

"There's a lot of self-loathing going on here," Lisa commented and eyed Chris in a concerned manner.

"It's warranted."

"Okay, so, say it is true that you did all that. Where do you go from here?" Lisa asked.

Chris put his head down as a lump formed in his throat. Tears began to fill his eyes as he conjured up the words he was about to speak. "I need to fix myself. This isn't the life I want to lead. I need to sober up, somehow, and work out my issues. That is not going to be easy, and it is not going to happen quickly. I don't trust myself not to mess up again. I don't trust myself not to hurt you. Being involved with me is dangerous."

"What are you saying?" Lisa asked and lowered her eyebrows.

Chris took a deep breath. "I'm saying I need to put you through a little bit of pain to save you from a lot of pain," he said.

"Are you breaking up with me?" she questioned him with a distressed look.

"Do everything in your power to forget about me. Block my phone number; block me online; go date someone else; do whatever you need to do to get over me. All I am going to do is let you down and cause you pain. You deserve more than I can give you right now. I love you so much, and that is why I can't continue to hurt you like this."

Lisa dropped her jaw and stared at him in silence. Tears filled her green eyes. She looked as though the wind had been knocked out of her. "No," she said in a firm tone. "You can do better; you can be better."

"Can I?" Chris asked. "I want to be, but do I believe I can? No. Not yet."

Lisa embraced Chris. "Let me be there for you; let me help you."

Chris hugged Lisa tightly. He hated the thought of losing her, of not being able to hold her, of not being able to confide in her, but more than anything, he hated the thought of hurting her over and over again. "I just don't trust myself," he admitted.

She grabbed ahold of his face and brought his lips to hers. As she kissed him, he began to wonder if she was right. *Did Marc and Jay exaggerate? Could she help me straighten out?* He thought that losing her could motivate him to straighten out and try to win her back. He ran his hand through her long brown hair and then pulled her down on top of him. As she began to kiss his neck and rub her body against his, Chris's stomach dropped. He could not continue to bring grief into her life. She needed a stable boyfriend, someone to help her heal—not someone who needed help of his own. "Lis," he said and pulled his neck away from her. "We can't fix this."

"You make me happier than anyone else," Lisa expressed. "Breaking up with me is what will shatter my heart into pieces."

Chris rested his head in his hands and tried to gather his thoughts. "I'm trying to avoid hurting you," he said.

"You've been through a lot in the last twenty-four hours," Lisa said and rubbed his shoulders. "Why don't you get some rest, think about things, and come over my house tomorrow after your baseball practice. We can talk more, once your head is clear."

Chris nodded. "Okay."

"I love you," Lisa said and kissed his forehead. "You're going to get through this."

"I want to."

"Chris," Lisa said and lifted his chin, "tell me you love me, too."

Chris looked Lisa in the eye. "I love you. That's why I'm so mad at myself. That's why this is so hard for me. I'm not used to having someone care about me."

"What are you talking about? All of your friends care about you. Marc, Jordan, and Taylor care about you. I'm sure, even in their own way, your parents love you, and Katie certainly cares about you."

"My friends would be fine without me. In fact, they'd probably be better off without me. Jon and Chantal would still be together if I hadn't talked Jon into drinking, and there wouldn't be dissention between Chantal and our whole group of friends. I ruin things for people."

"Jon is to blame for that mess—not you. Stop trying to take everything onto your shoulders," Lisa admonished him. "Jon is lying in the bed he made. Now you have to lie in yours—with or without me. That is for you to consider. I'm going to go home and try to get some sleep. Please, when you think about things, remember that I just want to be there for you, like you wanted to be there for me," she said sadly and put her head down. A few seconds later, she looked up at him with tears in her eyes. "Remember how horrible it felt when I shut you out? Please don't do that to me. I have no right to ask that, especially after pushing

108

you away, but I made a huge mistake, and we missed out on six months of being together."

"You have the right to ask me anything you want," Chris responded and brushed his hand against her cheek. "The sooner I get the help I need, the better off we will be."

Chapter 20

Lisa's head was spinning when she left Chris's house that evening. It was too late to call Cathy, Alyssa, Leslie, or Katherine for advice; she could not confide in either of her brothers about what had happened; she felt lost. *Even if my dad were alive, we couldn't talk about this. If there's a heaven, he's probably worried sick about me.* That possibility disturbed her.

When she arrived home, she went up to her bedroom and pulled out a journal in which she wrote her deepest thoughts. Turning to a blank page, she began writing herself a letter:

Lisa, what is wrong with you? You knew better than to get involved with Chris again. You knew he was an unstable mess and that you needed someone dependable. Why did you change your mind and go back out with him? All you have done is fall deeper in love with him over the past two months. See where following your heart gets you? If you hadn't been stupid enough to take molly, then you wouldn't have become so in tune with your feelings. Huge mistake. You let your guard down. Why? Is it because you're lonely, depressed, and heartbroken over your father? What is your problem? You sat there tonight begging a boy with a drug problem not to break up with you. Pitiful. But you did it out of love, so does that make it not so pitiful? You want to help him, right? Or are you just afraid to lose another person you trust? Why would you want to be tied down to someone with so much baggage? Entering high school as Chris's girlfriend would link you to his reputation, which could hurt your chances of being taken seriously by your teachers and peers. You want to be in student council. Why, oh, why did you let yourself fall in love with the life of the party?

Lisa closed her journal and took a deep breath. She was done scolding herself. Now, she needed to figure out a strategy to get what she wanted. She thought about the way losing Chantal put Andy and Jon on better paths. *Would losing me motivate Chris to straighten out? Probably,* she reasoned. *Ugh, I hate this.*

Chapter 21

The following afternoon, Marc dropped Chris off at Lisa's house. He was still hung over and full of self-hatred. When Lisa greeted him at the door, her disposition was remarkably different from the previous night.

"Hey, come in," she said and stepped aside to let him into her kitchen.

"Hi. How was your day?" Chris asked, reaching forward to hug her. She hugged him back but not tightly.

"It was okay; I guess," Lisa replied and pulled free from his embrace. "Let's go talk in my room. JC will be home from work soon, and he can't know what we are talking about."

Chris followed Lisa through her home in silence, dreading the conversation they were about to have. He could tell by the coldness of her demeanor that he had deeply hurt her. When they got to her bedroom, she sat at her desk and motioned for Chris to sit on her bed.

"You were right last night," she said and looked him directly in the eye. "I can't handle being with someone who has a drug problem. You need to get better before we can be together—if we're ever going to be together again."

Chris put his head down. "Don't wait for that to happen," he said. "As much as I want to believe we will be together again, I don't have enough faith in myself to ask you to wait for me." He looked up at Lisa and hoped that she could see in his eyes how much he truly cared for her.

Lisa dropped her eyes to the floor and nodded. "I won't. If I were to wait for you, then you would feel more pressure, which is the last thing you need right now."

"There are so many guys who want to date you," Chris said. "Find a good one and be happy. That's what you deserve."

"Chris, you are a good one. You've just gotten into some stuff that's messed you up; that's all."

"I haven't been sober one day in the last year," he admitted, "unless you count yesterday and today."

"You should cut people who do drugs out of your life," Lisa advised. "Stop talking to Luke. Block his number. Honestly, you should even distance yourself from Cathy and Jay."

"Why Cathy and Jay?"

"They're trying out all sorts of pills to treat her depression, and who knows where that will lead them? They both have good heads on their shoulders, but it's easier to get addicted to things than either one of them thinks."

"Well, Jay's definitely addicted to Adderall, but he's been prescribed it since he was in, like, third grade."

Lisa cocked her head to the side. "I didn't know he took Adderall. He has ADHD?"

Chris nodded. "Supposedly. I think he's just so smart that he gets bored in school, but his parents and doctor think he has ADHD. Without telling his parents, he stopped taking Adderall last year to see how well he could do. He got straight A's."

"He stopped taking it? I thought you just said he's addicted to it?" Lisa asked.

"All I am trying to say is that Jay's Adderall use isn't going to cause me to stumble," Chris explained.

"So, he takes it again?"

Chris sighed. "This conversation is not supposed to be about Jay."

"You're not shooting straight with me, so something more is going on with that," Lisa said flatly.

"Forget that I said anything about Adderall. My point is I don't think I need to distance myself from Jay or Cathy. Luke? Definitely— but not any of our close friends. I'm the bad influence in our group."

"Luke's not doing anyone any favors. I don't get why he's dealing drugs. He's rich; he doesn't need the money."

"He thinks he's helping people."

"I doubt he thinks that after what happened to you over the weekend."

Chris raised his eyebrows. "Yeah. I'm sure he feels pretty bad about that, but he had no idea I took Xanax, and he didn't know how much beer I drank."

"I can't believe Marc told you to do coke. Do you think he's done it before?"

Chris shook his head. "No way. He's seen it sober Taylor up a bunch of times, so he thought it would help me. He made a panicked decision. I know he feels bad about it now."

"I had no idea Taylor was into drugs like that," Lisa commented.

"Taylor's no angel," Chris stated matter-of-factly. "I bet he's done worse drugs than Jordan, yet he rags on Jordan for being a pothead."

"Jordan started in a couple football games," Lisa said. "I'd say he's doing better than Taylor."

"He's living Taylor's dream, and I think that's adding to Taylor's depression."

"Okay, so, enough about them… and Jay… and Cathy. Let's get back to *you*. Are you going to tell your parents?"

"I have to. Marc's parents will if I don't."

"Do you really think he's going to tell his parents? He might have said that to scare you into telling yours. They would be pretty upset if they found out he gave you coke."

"He'll tell them I ended up in the hospital because I drank on Xanax, but he's not going to tell them about anything else," Chris said and shook his head. "I don't really expect much help from my parents. They'll probably offer to send me away to a treatment program. I don't want to do that. I don't think I need detox because I don't think I'm addicted to anything. I just hate how I feel when I'm dead sober. I need to find the will to deal with my issues instead of getting high every day."

"Are you going to quit smoking weed?" Lisa asked.

"Not yet. It's pills I need to stay away from."

"What about drinking?"

Chris shrugged. "I'm going to see how things go. If I'm not an alcoholic, then I should be able to have a few beers and stop. But, who knows? I might be an alcoholic. It does run in my family."

"I can tell you've put some thought into this," Lisa said. "I'm not going to wait for you, but I'm always going to care about you. I'll do what you said. I'll block your number and block you online. I'll do my best to get over you. We can touch base next year when we're at the same school, and who knows? Maybe by then things will be different."

"I hate the idea of not talking to you every day, but I want you to do whatever is going to make this easier for you," Chris explained. "If it's easier for you to stay in my life as a friend, I am open to that. I just can't be a good boyfriend right now."

"I think it might be easier for me if we take a complete break," Lisa admitted. "I won't come to your parties or stalk your Instagram. I'll retreat to my friends from Sterling, and I'll be okay."

Chris nodded. "I'm so sorry, Lis."

"I know," Lisa said and smiled slightly.

"One more kiss and one more hug?" Chris asked and raised his eyebrows at her.

Lisa sighed. "That's so against my better judgement," she said as she got up from her chair and walked over to her bed. She sat down beside Chris and looked into his eyes.

"I understand if you don't want me to touch you," Chris said.

Without warning, Lisa threw her arms tightly around him. "I love you so much," she said with her voice cracking.

"I love you too," Chris said as tears welled up inside his eyes.

She ran her fingers along his cheek before gently pressing her lips against his. Then she rested her forehead against his and sighed. "The best moments of my life have been with you," she admitted.

"Same," Chris said while resting his head against hers.

She hugged him again and rested her head on his shoulder. He tried his best to savor the moment, wondering how often he would look back on it with regret over breaking up with her. They sat together for another few minutes, neither wanting to let go of the other first. If JC hadn't come home and knocked on Lisa's bedroom door, Chris doubted he would have ever been able to let go of her.

When he left Lisa's that night, Chris felt emptier than he could ever remember feeling. All that did was make him want to get high, but he knew in the long run, that would just prolong his misery. He walked all the way home from her house—six miles—lost in thought, trying to figure out where to go from there.

When he got home, he called Jason and told him everything that had happened. Jay promised to do whatever he could to help Chris get sober, but deep down inside, Chris knew Lisa had been right: Jason liked getting high just as much as Chris did. If he really wanted to straighten out, then he needed to surround himself with his straightedge friends.

After he hung up with Jason, he called Jon. He did not tell Jon about what had happened to him Saturday night or mention that he had ended up going to the hospital. However, he did tell Jon that all the concern he had shown for him in seventh grade had been warranted. Without exposing the list of drugs he had tried, he admitted that he had a problem. He also explained that he broke up with Lisa because he was afraid he would keep hurting her.

"I'm sorry, guy," Jon said compassionately. "Lisa's a great girl, and I know you're in love. You did the right thing, though. I should have broken up with Chantal when I needed to work through my issues. We probably would have been back together by now. I just needed some time to figure myself out, and instead of letting her go, I caused her a lot of pain. I ruined our relationship. So, believe me when I say you're doing the right thing."

Chris took a deep breath. "I needed to hear that," he stated appreciatively.

"The quicker you work through your problems, the better the chance you'll have at getting back together with her," Jon reasoned. "Let that motivate you."

"Pray for me, okay?" Chris asked. "You still pray, right?"

"Not as often as I should, but yes," Jon replied. "I can do that."

"Thank you," Chris said wholeheartedly. "I'm really going to need it."

Chapter 22

Lisa called Cathy after Chris left her house and filled her in on their breakup. Despite being emotionally shot, Lisa had found Chris's comment about Adderall intriguing. She began to wonder if Cathy and Jason were doing more drugs than Cathy had admitted to or if, perhaps, Jay was hiding something from Cathy.

"I'm sad that you two broke up," Cathy said in an awkwardly flat tone after Lisa explained why they had ended things. "You've been a good influence on him over the last two months. I don't understand why he would let you go."

"Have I really been a good influence?" Lisa questioned her. "I turned a blind eye to the pills he was taking. I thought I was being a good influence on him because he stopped drinking, but I clearly did not make much of an impact. If I had, he wouldn't have gotten drunk when I was at my cousin's wedding."

"True," Cathy agreed. "I'm kind of surprised he's taking this so seriously. I mean, Jay told me how serious it was, but I didn't expect Chris to break up with you over it."

Lisa sighed. "I just hope his parents step in and show him that they care. Perhaps he is subconsciously acting out to get their attention."

"How does he plan to get sober?"

"I have no idea," Lisa replied. "Marc wants him to join a teen recovery program. Chris said he doesn't want to go away for treatment, so I don't know what he's going to do. I have to stop myself from thinking about it if I want to get over him."

"Jay's going to try to help him," Cathy said. "He's worried."

"Do you really think Jay can help him? I know he doesn't drink, but he's not sober."

"Well, he's soberer than Chris," Cathy retorted.

"What has Jay told you he's done for drugs?"

"Why are you asking that?"

"Because Chris is probably going to cling to his straightedge friends right now, and I am curious how deep into drugs Jay has gotten."

"Deep into drugs?" Cathy asked, sounding surprised. "He only smokes weed. I'm technically deeper into drugs than him."

"That's not true. He tripped with Chris a few times, and he tried the pills you take for anxiety."

"He hates benzos. He only took them so he could tell me what to expect. I was scared to take them."

"But he wasn't scared? Don't you find that odd?"

"What are you implying?"

"Jay knows you have anxiety. I'm sure he would hide things from you that he thought would upset you. He's Chris's very best friend. I would not be surprised if he has tried other things with Chris that you don't know about. That's all."

"You think my boyfriend does drugs behind my back?"

"I don't know. I'm just saying it's a possibility because his brother is a drug dealer; he didn't hesitate to try out those pills for you; and Chris is his best friend," Lisa reasoned.

"Well, he turned down painkillers the other night when Luke offered them to us," Cathy commented, "so I don't think I have anything to worry about."

"It doesn't bother you when he trips?"

"Yeah, it bothers me," Cathy admitted, "but he doesn't do it much. I'd rather him eat mushrooms occasionally than drink at every party."

"I think you should ask him to be honest with you about everything he's tried," Lisa pressed.

"Why are you prodding me? What did Chris tell you?"

"He said he doesn't think being around Jay will cause him to stumble," Lisa replied, "so that's good. He just mentioned something about ADHD medicine."

119

"Oh," Cathy said flatly. "Jay told me he was prescribed Adderall for four or five years. I thought you were talking about recreational drugs, so I didn't mention it. He stopped taking Adderall last year because he didn't think he needed it."

"Chris said something that made me think he might be taking it again."

"Oh, really?" Cathy asked, sounding rather careless. "Well, maybe this year is harder than last year? Maybe he needs more help focusing? His parents will only let him attend MLH if he gets straight A's, so he's under a lot of pressure. He could be taking it again. I have no idea."

"Have you read up on Adderall at all?"

"No."

"Well, I did after Chris told me he tried it. And guess what? If people don't need it, it gets them high. Chris doesn't think Jay has ADHD. He thinks he just has a really high IQ and gets bored easily."

"He does have a high IQ. It's, like, over 140 or something," Cathy stated matter-of-factly, "and he does get bored easily."

"So, he could have been misdiagnosed."

"Yeah, or he has ADHD *because* he gets bored easily, *because* he has a genius IQ," Cathy remarked. "His parents had a full neuro-psych evaluation done on him."

"Well, then, maybe he really does need Adderall. I don't know. I just wanted to bring it to your attention because it came up in our conversation today."

"Is Chris worried about Jay or something?" Cathy asked.

"No! Not at all!" Lisa exclaimed. "I'm sorry. I'm not trying to worry you. I was just caught off guard when Chris mentioned Adderall to me because I didn't know Jay ever took it."

"I don't care if he takes Adderall. I want him to do whatever he needs to do to get straight A's so we can go to high school together," Cathy said. "If his behavior had changed, then I would be concerned, but he's the same as he's always been."

"I think his behavior has changed a little," Lisa commented. "I think weed has mellowed him out a bit."

"Yeah, maybe," Cathy said, again sounding unconcerned. "I hardly see him during the week because he's so bogged down with schoolwork, but he told me he's been smoking it almost every day."

"Do you only smoke weed when you're with him?"

"I've never done it alone," Cathy replied. "I wouldn't need to because I don't get anxiety when I'm by myself."

"Do you get anxiety around Jay?"

"Not when it's just the two of us."

"Interesting."

"What are you getting at?" Cathy questioned her. "I know you're upset because you just lost your relationship with Chris to drugs, but you don't have to worry about me or Jason."

"Okay," Lisa said and let out a heavy breath. "You're right. I'm probably being paranoid because of what happened between Chris and me. I didn't see it coming. Usually, I can see where things are headed. This blindsided me."

"Well, love is blind," Cathy said matter-of-factly.

After Lisa finished talking to Cathy, she reflected on their conversation. Something about Cathy's nonchalant tone gave her an uneasy feeling. Lisa had expected Cathy to show more concern for Chris than she had, as well as more sympathy for her. *Perhaps, she's just tired.* Cathy was not an overly emotional person, which was one reason why Lisa liked her so much. Even so, she was not careless by any means. She, like Lisa, usually enjoyed reading into things and exploring theories. That night, however, she seemed unfazed by everything Lisa had mentioned.

Chapter 23

***

May of 2017

One month after Lisa and Chris's breakup, Chantal caught Cathy and Jason smoking pot in the Kagellis' backyard and confronted them. After Chantal stormed off angrily, Cathy realized it would likely heighten the wall of separation between them. Chantal's cross tone made Cathy feel judged and misunderstood.

After Jason left that evening, Chantal barged into Cathy's room. "I can't believe you guys smoke weed now!" she cried in dismay. "You were so hard on Jon for trying it!"

Cathy rolled her eyes. "I was hard on Jon for getting drunk and hiding it from you."

"Why would you ever smoke pot?" Chantal asked and shut Cathy's door.

"I like it," Cathy replied. "It calms my mind."

Chantal looked away in disgust.

"I've been having panic attacks lately, and weed keeps them at bay," Cathy added.

Chantal turned toward Cathy and glared at her. "Do you drink now, too? Does that also 'calm your mind'?"

"Don't mock me," Cathy said. "I'm being honest with you about an issue I'm having—and no, I don't drink."

Chantal crossed her arms. "How do you not feel guilty about doing drugs? It's a sin."

"I don't consider weed a drug," Cathy replied. "It's a natural way to treat my anxiety."

Chantal shook her head. "It's a drug, Cathy. It can lead to the use of other drugs. Mom and Dad would be devastated if they found out about this."

"Well, they won't find out if you keep your mouth shut," Cathy commented matter-of-factly. "Like, how I never told Mom anything about Jon."

Chantal let out a heavy breath. "I'm not going to tell on you, but I'm worried about you. This isn't like you, and I didn't think it was like Jason either."

"Chantal, you have no idea what is 'like me' or what is 'like Jason' because you shut us out of your life," Cathy rebuked.

"So, does everyone smoke pot now? Jon? Alyssa? Bryan? Everyone?!" Chantal asked, appearing deeply bothered.

"No," Cathy replied. She did not feel the need to elaborate because Chantal did not deserve an explanation. What everyone did was none of her business.

"Why are you being so cold toward me?"

"Cold?" Cathy questioned her with a short laugh. "I'm not being cold; I just don't care anymore. I tried for months to fix things between us, and caring about our relationship nearly drove me insane. So, I learned how to stop caring."

Chantal's eyes filled with tears. "All you had to do was stop being friends with Alyssa," she retorted.

"I'm not having this conversation again," Cathy said and walked over toward her door. "Are we done? Can you leave? Please?"

Chantal widened her eyes, clearly taken aback by Cathy's attitude. "What is wrong with you?" she asked before turning to leave the room.

"Nothing. I'm just done trying to be your friend," Cathy replied honestly while opening her bedroom door. "Please leave," she added. She could tell by the look on Chantal's face that she was stunned. Cathy had recently decided that she needed to protect herself from her twin because after nearly eight months Chantal had refused to reconcile with her. For once, Cathy had been able to shut off her empathy and freely speak her mind. She didn't feel the need to take care of Chantal's feelings; in fact, she didn't feel much of anything at all. That was the day the tables turned in their relationship, when Cathy finally felt like she had some control over the situation.

Chapter 24

Shortly after Chantal left Cathy's room, Cathy called Jason to tell him about their conversation. "You're pretending you don't care because you think she doesn't," Jason said after Cathy explained everything to him.

"No," Cathy stated firmly. "I really just don't care."

"Well, that's good… I guess," Jason commented in an uneasy tone. "But she is your sister, so if she tries to make up with you, you should still be open to it."

"I'm done getting my hopes up about that."

"Are you mad at her for judging you?"

"No."

"Well, then where did this attitude adjustment come from?"

"I don't know. I think maybe I've finally learned how to shut off the thing inside of me that makes me put myself in other people's shoes. My whole life, I've made it a priority not to hurt other people's feelings and to avoid conflict. It's exhausting," Cathy explained. "That's why I admire Lisa's ability to be forthright and even selfish at times. I've never been able to do that."

"Your kind heart is one of your most attractive traits," Jason said. "Don't harden up because Chantal has been cold to you or because your best friend is kind of a brat."

"Lisa's *not* a brat. I thought you would be proud of me for finally standing up to Chantal," Cathy stated with annoyance.

"I am," Jason said. "It's a huge step for you, and I think caring less about your relationship with her will be good for you. I'm just curious about where this new perspective has come from."

Cathy sighed. "Please don't try to psychoanalyze me right now."

"I'm not," Jason responded defensively. "I'm just trying to understand you better."

"I think I explained myself pretty clearly."

Jason let out a heavy breath. "You did. I'm sorry. I'm just surprised; that's all."

Cathy realized she needed to lighten the mood or they could easily end up getting in an argument. "Well, taking you by surprise every once in a while is a good thing," she said in a cheerful tone. "I wouldn't want you to ever get bored with me."

Jason laughed. "I don't think I could ever get bored with you."

"When are your parents going to start spending their weekends in Newport?" Cathy asked, purposely changing the subject. "It's getting pretty nice out."

"Memorial Day weekend. They'll go down and open up our house. I can't wait. Only two more weeks of class for me."

"Lucky. We're stuck going through the end of June because of all the snow days."

"Well, it's my last year of getting out early because I'm pretty certain I pulled off straight A's this term," Jason stated proudly.

"I never doubted you would!"

"My parents have already met with the guidance department at Montgomery Lake High to figure out what classes I would be enrolled in. I'm a bit ahead of the normal curriculum, so they're going to place me in level zero classes and allow me to take some AP courses with older kids."

"Again, I'm not surprised."

"So, it's really happening. I'm finally going to be at the same school as you and Chris and everyone."

"You've certainly worked for it," Cathy remarked.

"Oh, I was thinking. I don't think we should go to Newport every weekend this summer," Jason stated. "My parents are allowing Matt to stay home because he wants to spend the summer with his Montgomery friends, so he'll be able to babysit me. I feel like we grew apart from our friends while we were gone last summer."

"I love Newport, but that's fine," Cathy said.

"Part of the reason is that I want to be here for Chris."

"I figured that much."

"He misses Lisa a lot, and I'm afraid he'll turn back to pills if I'm not around to distract him."

"She misses him too, but she's been distracting herself with another guy. I think she's shut down her ability to feel anything at this point. After losing her dad and then Chris breaking up with her, she's just functioning on autopilot. This new kid, Jeff, isn't going to get to her heart; she's done letting people in."

"That's not good, but I honestly don't blame her," Jason commented. "She's been traumatized."

"Right? So, don't ever call her a brat again."

Jason laughed. "I'm sorry. You know I love Lisa."

"I just wish she still hung out with our friends."

"I'm not against hanging out with Lisa's group of friends."

"Really? Well, then maybe we can make plans with them. It would just be awkward if Andy and Chantal were there. I'm pretty sure they think we are terrible people—especially now that Chantal knows we smoke pot."

"We could just hang out with Lisa and Jeff," Jason suggested. "Honestly, Chris is not going to hold it against me. He's not Jon."

Chapter 25

On the following day, Cathy set off to make plans with Lisa to get Jeff and Jason acquainted. "Wouldn't that be weird?" Lisa asked, raising her eyebrows in surprise.

"No. Jay's fine with it. I told him that I missed having you hang out with us, so he suggested that we double date."

"Okay, well, I'll see if Jeff is open to the idea," Lisa replied with a shrug.

Jeff, being socially inclined, was excited to expand his social circle and spend time with Cathy and Jason. Over the following month, he and Jason developed a bromance, built upon their mutual love for teasing people. Cathy could understand why Lisa was attracted to Jeff: he looked as much like a model as she did. He had been persistent in his pursuit of her, despite multiple setbacks, and for that reason she felt safe with him. He was involved in student council, and he was a great student-athlete. Jeff was everything Lisa had said she wanted earlier that year.

Aside from Jeff and Leslie, the rest of Lisa's friends chose to keep their distance from Cathy and Jason. Lisa told Cathy that because Andy, Chantal, Bobby, Adam, and Katherine were straightedge, they didn't want to be associated with kids who did drugs. Cathy took offense to that because she didn't consider her group of friends to be "druggies." Chris was trying his best to straighten out; Jon was back in anti-drug mode; Alyssa was forbidden by Jon from experimenting with anything; and Bryan, who would occasionally drink, made it clear that drugs were not for him. Cathy assumed that Chantal had painted them all in a bad light. Otherwise, she couldn't comprehend why they would think poorly of her friends.

"I told everyone that you guys are awesome," Jeff said one early summer evening at Jason's house with Lisa and Cathy. "Bobby and

128

Katherine can be kind of stuck up; Adam's quiet. I wouldn't take it personally."

"I'm sure my sister hasn't helped our case," Cathy stated dryly and rolled her eyes. She paused before taking a hit off a joint Jason had passed her. They were outside smoking on his deck—in no risk of getting in trouble because his parents were in Rhode Island.

"Chantal doesn't say much," Jeff commented as he watched Lisa take the joint from Cathy. "Since when do *you* smoke weed?" he questioned her.

Lisa shrugged and then took a hit off the joint. "Don't tell Andy," she said after she exhaled.

"Bullshit!" Jeff exclaimed and laughed. "You gave us both so much crap for smoking. Now you smoke weed?"

"Here. Try it," Lisa said and offered the joint to Jeff.

Cathy raised her eyebrows, wondering if he would try it.

"I'm all set," Jeff said and waved off Lisa's hand, "but you can't give me crap if I ever decide to smoke a cigarette again."

"Yes, I can!" Lisa cried and passed the joint to Jason.

Jeff laughed and shook his head.

"When did Andy ever smoke?" Cathy asked, wondering if he was hiding that from her sister.

Jeff rolled his eyes. "Lisa freaked out on us for trying it a couple years ago. I don't think either one of us ever did it again."

"Yup!" Lisa exclaimed happily. "Smoking is disgusting."

"Says the girl who now smokes weed?" Jeff asked and cocked his head to the side.

Lisa nodded. "It's different—it's not a habit; and it doesn't smell bad; and it's not physically addictive."

"Whatever you need to tell yourself," Jeff commented with a smirk and a twinkle in his eye.

"None of our friends can know!" Lisa stated and looked pleadingly into Jeff's eyes. "They'll judge me."

"They won't judge you for anything. They know you've been through a lot," Jeff said and wrapped his arms around her.

"Trust me," Lisa said and hugged him back. "Katherine, Adam, Bobby, and Andy will have a problem with it. Leslie won't care, but she has a big mouth, and she'll tell everyone else."

"Fine," Jeff acquiesced. "My lips are sealed."

"Here," Jason said to Cathy as he offered her the joint.

"I'm good," Cathy replied. She was nervous about smoking weed that night because she had also taken Xanax. She had no idea how the two drugs were going to interact.

"Lisa?" Jason asked.

Lisa took the joint from him and held it up to Jeff. "Just take one hit," she pleaded. "You won't even get high because it's your first time."

"Lis, lay off him," Jason spoke up. "He'll try it sometime if he wants to."

Lisa sighed. "Fine," she said before taking another hit and passing it back to Jason.

Cathy was fully aware of everything that was happening around her, and she wanted to stick up for Jeff, but she couldn't speak. She had a mental block. It was the strangest feeling; it felt as though there was a wall up in her brain, restricting access to her vocabulary.

Jason put the joint under his foot and stomped on it. "I'll be right back," he said and then walked down the steps into his backyard. Cathy hoped he would hurry. She needed to sit down as soon as possible. "Relaxed" was not even an adequate way to describe how she felt; "mentally asleep" was more like it. Lisa and Jeff were kissing each other against the railing while Cathy stared off into the yard, looking for her boyfriend.

"Are you okay?" Jason asked once he returned. He placed his hand on Cathy's shoulder and looked into her eyes. Cathy shook her head from side to side. "Are you going to be sick?" he asked. Cathy shook her head again. She felt as though she was looking at her boyfriend through a tunnel. The air around her seemed thick, and everything was shaking. She began to wonder if she was having a panic attack, but she noticed her palms were not sweating. "Well, what's wrong with you?" Jason asked, staring at her with concern.

She steadied herself against Jason's house and let out a heavy breath. "I need to lie down," she managed to express.

"Oh, babe, you're stoned," Jason said and threw his arm around her shoulders. "Let's go inside. We can put on a movie, and you can lie down."

Cathy nodded and followed Jason inside while holding onto the back of his shirt. Once they reached the family room, she flopped down on the couch before Jason even had time to turn on the TV. When she closed her eyes, she felt as though she were somersaulting through the air.

"Cathy, come lie down with me," she heard Jason say. She did nothing to acknowledge that she had heard him, but a few seconds later, she felt him pull her body towards his. He positioned a pillow beneath her head and then ran his hand through her hair in a soothing manner.

The next thing Cathy knew, she was waking up alone in pitch blackness. She jumped up, wondering where she was. The only light coming into the room was starlight from the large palladium window to her left. As her eyes began to adjust, she realized she was alone in Jason's family room. Where were Lisa, Jeff, and Jason? She squinted to read the clock on the cable box. It was 3:15 a.m.! Cathy widened her eyes and dropped her jaw. She had slept for nearly six hours?!

Cathy stood up from the couch and felt her way over to the light switch. After turning on the family room and hallway lights, she cautiously made her way into Jason's foyer. The house was completely still while she climbed up the stairs that led to the second floor. Tiptoeing past Matt's bedroom, Cathy reached Jason's room undetected. She did not hesitate before whipping open the door and turning on the light. She softly closed the door behind her and then walked over to Jason's bed. "Jay, wake up! Why aren't I at Lisa's?" she asked frantically.

"Ah!" Jason cried, startled as he came out of sleep. He took a deep breath. "Oh good. You're awake."

"What happened?!" she questioned him with protruding eyes.

"When Lisa's brother got here, we couldn't wake you up," Jason replied while pushing over and motioning for Cathy to climb into his bed.

"Did you guys even try?"

"Yes!" Jason cried with a short laugh. "Lisa was afraid her brother would call your mom if you didn't go home with her, so we tried a bunch of times, but you were out cold. Lisa told him you went home sick."

"Why did you leave me downstairs in the dark?"

"Matt came home and told me to go to bed. He said you weren't getting pregnant on his watch."

Cathy, who was still standing by the bed, dropped her jaw. "He thinks we're sleeping together?!"

"Relax," Jason said with a short laugh. "He was just teasing me."

"So, he can't know I'm up here?"

"His new girlfriend is in his bed right now. He won't tell on me if I don't tell on him, so you really have nothing to worry about."

"What did you say was wrong with me?"

"I told him the truth," Jason replied. "I told him we smoked weed and you passed out from it because you have a low tolerance."

"You told him?!"

"Matt already knows I smoke. He caught me a couple months ago."

"I'm so embarrassed," she said as she slumped onto Jason's bed beside him.

"Don't be," Jason said carelessly. "Matt isn't going to hold it against you; he'll hold it against me for corrupting you."

"How am I going to get home?" Cathy asked. "Ugh. Am I going to have to lie to my parents?"

"I already convinced Matt to drive you to Lisa's in the morning before your mom gets there. It's all worked out."

"Won't her brothers think it's weird that I'm getting dropped off just to get picked up by my mother?"

"Lisa said JC and Joe are both leaving for the office before 8:00 a.m."

Cathy let out a sigh of relief. "Okay, that's good. My mom is picking me up at 10:30." Feeling a bit more relaxed, she lay down in the bed.

Jason pulled his baby blue down comforter over her and pulled her body close to his. "After fifteen months, I finally got you in my bed!" he happily proclaimed.

Cathy rolled over to face him. "Good job," she said with a short laugh.

He brushed the back of his hand against her cheek. "Why do you think you passed out for so long?" he questioned her. "I told Matt you have a low tolerance, but that's not really true. I've never seen anyone get that messed up from one hit of weed."

"I took Xanax before I came over," Cathy admitted.

Jason widened his blue eyes. "Oh, crap! No one should drink or smoke on Xanax. It will mess you up."

"Clearly," Cathy said and widened her eyes.

"I thought you only took that when you were having a panic attack," Jason said and stared into her eyes.

"I've been taking it more often because I've realized it helps me not care about things," she admitted.

"How often?" Jason asked.

Cathy shrugged. "Before social events, before assemblies at school, before dealing with Chantal…"

Jason lowered his eyebrows. "Do you take it every day? How much did Luke give you?"

"No, not every day," Cathy replied. "He gave me a bunch of it."

133

Jason cocked his head to the side. "How long have you been doing this?" His concern was evident in both his eyes and his tone.

"Luke gave it to me in April, a couple days after Chris almost overdosed. He felt bad that I got sick from the Vicodin, so he gave me a whole bottle."

"Why didn't you tell me?"

Cathy could not tell if he was surprised or angry. She shrugged. "I guess it just didn't come up in conversation."

"Babe, Xanax is really addictive, and you can develop a tolerance fast," Jason warned her. "You shouldn't take it every day unless you're prescribed it by a doctor."

"Like you're prescribed Adderall?" she asked and raised her eyebrows. She gazed at him curiously, wondering if he had anything to say on the matter.

Jason squinted at her and then said, "Yeah, like I'm prescribed Adderall."

"Do you take it?" she questioned him.

"Yeah," he replied. "I started taking it again when I was studying for midterms."

"You're out of school now, but you still take it?"

"I take it every day like my parents want me to," Jason responded.

"You told me you don't need it and that you don't think you have ADHD."

"Right. Then when I was trying to get A's on all my midterms, I realized I was much more productive when I took it. Even though I'm not in school right now, I still want to be productive."

"But if you don't need it, doesn't it get you high?" Cathy asked. "Have you read up on it?"

"No. I just know it's an amphetamine."

"I feel better on it, so maybe I was wrong? Maybe I do have ADHD? Maybe I do need it? I don't know. Maybe I pulled off straight A's in seventh grade without it because the curriculum was easy? I don't

134

ask myself these types of questions because Adderall is something my parents have been telling me to take since I was eight years old."

"You're right; it's different," Cathy concluded. "I'm not prescribed Xanax. I get it from your brother, not a pharmacy."

Jason searched her eyes. "What do you feel like when you're on it? How do you function? It made me fall asleep."

"That's probably because you don't have anxiety, so it calmed you to the point of slumber. It just makes me feel comfortable to do and say whatever I want. It keeps me from over-analyzing things. It helps me stay out of my head."

"See, I get distracted by outer stimuli, and Adderall helps me focus. You get distracted by your own thoughts and feelings, so that's probably why Xanax helps you."

"You can't be mad at me for taking Xanax if you take Adderall every day," Cathy said and gave him her sad eyes. "They're both addictive," she added.

"Did you just admit to taking it every day?"

Cathy smiled slightly. "No," she replied.

"Please be careful," he said and kissed her forehead.

"I won't smoke weed when I'm on it," she promised. "I never want what happened to me tonight to happen again."

"I don't either, but I'm happy you're in my bed!" Jason exclaimed and rolled over so that he was on top of her. "I'm going to shut off the light," he said before rolling off of his bed and hustling to the light switch. Everything went dark, and Cathy could not see him as he approached the bed. She felt his hand on her shoulder. "Push over," he said and slid into bed next to her.

"I can't believe I'm sleeping in your bed," Cathy stated. "Neither one of us planned this."

"I know, right? How lucky am I?" he laughed.

She felt him wrap his arms around her and pull her fully-clothed body closer into his. "Good night," he said and kissed the back of her head.

"Good night," she replied and kissed his arm.

Chapter 26

A few days later, Marc drove Jason, Luke, and Chris to Plymouth for the Fourth of July. Jon's relatives owned a house on Saquish Beach, and Jon had invited everyone to camp out overnight. Cathy was not allowed to go because her parents did not want her sleeping in a tent with boys. Alyssa had not been allowed to attend for the same reason. However, Bryan was supposedly bringing Courtney. Evidently she had family nearby, whose house her parents would be visiting. They had agreed to drop her and Bryan off and pick them up later that evening. Jason was the only one of their friends who had ever met Courtney, and it had only been in passing at the mall one day.

"I wish Jordan let you take his Jeep," Chris said on the long drive southeast. "It's so cramped back here." He, Jason, the tent bag, and all their backpacks were stuffed into the backseat of Marc's truck.

"I'm sure he would have if I didn't have four-wheel drive," Marc commented.

"Not hating on Jordan anymore?" Chris asked, sounding surprised.

Marc glanced at Chris in his rearview mirror. "Not loving him either."

Chris smirked.

"How many people did Jon invite?" Luke asked, turning toward Chris.

"He invited everyone we hang out with, but since it's over an hour away, not that many people are coming from Montgomery," Chris replied. "I think a lot of his cousins will be there. It should still be a good time."

"Saquish Beach? On the Fourth? Definitely," Luke stated assuredly.

"His mom's wicked strict, so if you plan on drinking, you'll have to hide it in a solo cup," Chris said.

"Oh, we brought them," Luke said, "and a big bottle of Fireball."

Chris began laughing. "Is that why you're not hating on Jordan, Marky?"

Marc smirked. "Something like that."

"Are you going to drink tonight?" Chris asked, while turning toward Jason.

Jason shrugged. "Cathy's not here, so I could. I don't know. I think I'd rather just get baked."

"No!" Luke exclaimed. "You are not escaping the night without taking a shot with me."

***

Later that evening, Jason watched from his seat at the bonfire as Bryan and Courtney approached them. Bryan had told Jason that he was scared their friends would frighten Courtney away, but because Jon's mother was so strict, he assumed the party would not get out of control. Bryan had been right; so far, Jason was having a very chill night. There was a bonfire located every fifty feet down the beach, and people were mingling from one to the next. Jon's family was scattered around them, but no one seemed suspicious of any kids drinking.

Earlier, Jason and Chris had gone for a walk down the beach and smoked a bowl without Jon's mother noticing. Jason was still slightly high when he saw Courtney sit down next to Bryan on a log. She was hot. With shoulder-length black hair, bright blue eyes, and a petite figure, Courtney was just as beautiful as any of the other girls they hung out with. After meeting her at the mall, he understood why Bryan had been so persistent in his pursuit of her. She was not only beautiful, but also classy. She had a bright air about her that Jason found attractive. He was happy that Bryan had finally won her heart. Courtney had been with Bryan for roughly a year and a half, so meeting Jon and Chris was long overdue. Jason nudged Chris. "Courtney's hot, huh?" he said and widened his eyes.

"She's all right," Chris replied.

"That's Mayor Angeletti's daughter," Jason stated. "She's more than all right, dude! I'd capitalize on her in a second if she weren't dating Sartelli. Now we know why he kept her hidden for so long." Of course, he had meant if he were single.

Chris said nothing in response for a moment and then suddenly stood up from his seat. "I need to go talk to her."

Jason looked up at Chris in surprise and then slowly rose to meet his best friend. "All right, guy. I'll introduce you," he offered, leading Chris over to where Courtney was seated.

She looked up and smiled at Jason as he appeared before her. "Hello, Courtney. This is Chris," he greeted her. "He's a friend of Bryan's, too."

"Yeah, he's the guy we go to when we want to have some *fun*," Bryan said as he stood up to slap hands with Chris and Jason.

"It's nice to meet you," Courtney replied softly, planting her eyes on Chris.

Chris smiled, nodded, and then walked away from them towards the Atlantic.

Bryan looked at Jason strangely.

"I think he's a little stoned," Jason remarked.

Bryan rolled his eyes, likely afraid that the news would bother Courtney.

"I'll be right back," Courtney announced suddenly and dashed off after Chris. Jason turned towards the ocean and saw Chris sitting in the sand near the water. Courtney ran over to him, smiled widely, and then sat down beside him.

"She's just really friendly," Bryan commented.

"I guess so," Jason stated in a tone that expressed how surprised he was. "Well, let's go over there. If you want a drink, Luke brought some hard liquor. He, Chris, and Marc have been taking shots of it all night."

"No, I'm all set," Bryan said as he walked with Jason towards the water. "I won't be drinking with her here. You're not drinking?"

Jason shook his head.

"Well, good. Courtney shouldn't feel too uncomfortable if you, me, and Jon are all not drinking," Bryan reasoned.

Jason patted Bryan on the back. "We're not going to scare your girlfriend away, buddy. Relax."

"Hey!" Courtney exclaimed vibrantly as Jason and Bryan approached her and Chris. "It's so nice down here by the water. The wet sand feels so good beneath my toes. I usually only get to go to the beach on vacation."

"It's a nice treat," Jason commented, wondering what Courtney had said to Chris and why she had rushed to his side.

"The weather's perfect," Chris said. "We'll have a clear sky for the fireworks. We should be in for a good night—as long as the barge doesn't explode like it did a couple years ago."

Jason began laughing. "I forgot about that."

Jon joined them by the water a moment later, and Bryan introduced him to Courtney. "I've heard so many good things about you," Jon said as he shook her hand. "We've all wanted you to hang out with us for a while."

"I've always wanted to come," Courtney expressed. "I just didn't have the invite," she added and eyed Bryan precariously.

"Do you guys want anything to eat or drink?" Jon asked. "There are burgers on the grill and a bunch of side dishes."

Courtney placed her hand on Jon's shoulder. "You're so nice. We went out for dinner with my parents before we came, so I'm good with food, but I'd love a water."

"You got it. Does anyone else want anything?" Jon asked before turning to walk up toward the house.

"Water," Jason replied.

"Me too," Chris added.

"I'll help you carry everything," Bryan offered. "Court, are you okay with that?"

Courtney nodded.

Once Bryan and Jon were out of hearing distance, Chris turned to Jason. "Do you want to smoke again?" he asked.

Jason widened his eyes. That was exactly what Bryan had not wanted Courtney to hear. According to Bryan, Courtney was a devout, evangelical Christian. After seeing the way Chantal had reacted to Jason and Cathy smoking weed, he assumed Courtney would take a similar stance. "I'm good," he replied.

"Do you want to smoke, Courtney?" Chris asked.

Jason let out a heavy breath as he watched Courtney try to find words.

"Drugs are against my religious beliefs," she said a few seconds later, sounding more apologetic than offended. "They don't interest me."

Chris nodded and smiled. "Okay then. I'm going for a walk by myself."

Once Chris was out of hearing distance, Courtney asked, "Was he talking about cigarettes or weed?"

"Oh, weed," Jason replied with a short laugh. "He would never ask me if I wanted a cigarette."

"Oh, okay. Well, I know Bryan sometimes smokes, so I didn't know if you all did."

Jason shook his head and smiled. "Jon and I definitely do not smoke cigarettes. I smoke weed; Jon smokes nothing."

Courtney nodded. "Bryan told me Jon was straightedge. He filled me in on all of you."

"Oh, boy," Jason gasped facetiously. "What did he tell you about me?"

"That you're in love with your girlfriend Cathy, and that you used to be a huge player before you met her," Courtney replied immediately.

Jason laughed. "Okay, I can take that."

"He warned me that you and Chris might be high," she added. "He told me that he's smoked weed with you guys before."

"Yeah, but Bryan hasn't done that in ages," Jason commented, wondering if Courtney was testing him.

"That's what he said, too."

Jason draped his arm around Courtney's shoulders. "Come on. Let's go up to the bonfire. There's a cold breeze coming off the water, and I can see you're shivering."

"Okay," Courtney agreed and walked alongside him until they reached the fire.

"Jon and Bryan are on their way back now," Jason said and pointed to his friends, who were carrying multiple bottles of water and bags of chips.

Suddenly, Jason heard Luke's voice calling his name over the loud chant of the bonfire. Jason turned to see what in the world his older brother was up to. He was waving Jason over to Marc's truck. "Oh, God," Jason muttered. "My older brother is trying to get me to drink with him."

Courtney turned to see Luke. "Your older brother is *hot*," she commented with wide eyes.

Jason smiled. Courtney was a lot more laidback than he had expected. He waved Luke off and turned back toward her. "He's not getting me drunk in front of Jon's family."

Courtney's eyes sparkled somewhat mischievously as she smiled back at him. "I'm just happy to finally be here. Bryan's kept me hidden for too long."

Chapter 27

On the following Saturday, Jason invited his close friends over to use his pool. Like everything at his house, it had been custom designed. The stone waterfall, slide, and adjacent tiki bar were some of its best features. His parents had recently wired the bar with cable, so Jason was happily lying on a lounge chair, casually watching baseball. Cathy and Alyssa were floating on a double raft in the pool while Lisa and Jeff were flirting with each other in the deep end. Jon was next to Jason on another lounge chair, closely watching the game, and Bryan was on his way.

"Is Sartelli bringing Courtney?" Jason asked, turning toward Jon.

"No idea. Hopefully."

"I like her," Jason said. "I feel bad that he kept her away from us for so long. I could tell by some of the things she said at Saquish that she had wanted to hang out with us all along."

"Well, I don't think we scared her off," Jon gathered.

Nevertheless, twenty minutes later, Bryan arrived without Courtney. He took a seat on the other side of Jason and pulled his shirt over his head. "Hey," he greeted them rather downheartedly.

"What's up, guy? No Courtney?" Jason asked and squinted as he glanced over at his friend.

Bryan, who had lain down and closed his eyes, shook his head.

"You have to start allowing her out more often," Jon prodded. "She's great."

Bryan opened his brown eyes and turned to face Jon. "She's being weird."

"Are you afraid Dunkin scared her off when he asked her to smoke pot?" Jason asked.

"She didn't even tell me about that," Bryan replied.

"Oh, well, then she must not have been too bothered by it," Jason reasoned.

"Yeah, I don't think we did anything to scare her away," Jon said. "You guys left before Jay started puking."

Jason rolled his eyes. "Shut up, dude," he said and shoved Jon in the shoulder.

Jon laughed.

"Did Luke make you drink?" Bryan asked.

Jason nodded. "He made me take a few shots with him. I forced myself to throw up so he would think I was sick and leave me alone. He was just happy that I drank with him before Matt."

"Did you tell Cathy?" Bryan asked and nodded toward her in the pool.

"She didn't care," Jason replied. "Nothing seems to faze her lately."

"That's crazy," Jon said. "She was harder on me than Chantal was when I drank last year."

"We've desensitized her," Jason stated. "I'm not sure if that's a good thing or a bad thing."

"Have you guys—?" Jon asked and raised his eyebrows at Jason.

"Have we what?" Jason questioned him.

"You know…" Jon implied.

"Banged?" Jason asked.

Jon nodded.

Jason shook his head and closed his eyes. "Not even close."

"Well, I guess she hasn't changed that much then," Jon remarked. "Bryan?"

"Courtney?" Bryan questioned him. "Are you kidding? If I marry her, I will get married as a virgin."

Jason and Jon both laughed. "Why are you asking about this?" Jason wondered, finding it odd that Jon brought up sex. "Have you and Alyssa been busy in that area lately?"

"Busy enough," Jon replied and nodded towards her.

144

"Good for you, buddy," Jason said and patted Jon on the shoulder. He reached into the little black bag he had brought from his house and pulled out a bag of weed, a lighter, and the glass bowl Chris had given him. "Do you guys want to smoke?" he asked, although knowing both of his friends would surely say no.

"No, but I can see your lighter?" Bryan asked and pulled a cigarette out of his pocket.

"You smoke?" Jason questioned him as he handed over the lighter. He had honestly forgotten that Bryan had ever smoked with Chris until Courtney brought it up on the Fourth of July.

"No. Not usually," Bryan replied and lit a cigarette.

Jason took back his lighter and brought it to the bowl he had just packed. "You should smoke this; it's better for you," he said before taking a hit.

"I shouldn't smoke anything," Bryan stated dryly.

"Why are you smoking?" Jon questioned him. "What's wrong with you today?"

"Courtney broke up with me," Bryan said without turning to look at Jon or Jason.

"What, dude?!" Jason exclaimed.

"Why?!" Jon cried.

"I don't know."

"C'mon, guy. You've got to give us more than that!" Jason pressed.

"She said she couldn't enter high school with her middle-school boyfriend," Bryan responded.

"Why not?" Jason asked.

"I have no idea," Bryan replied. "It came out of nowhere. She said she needed 'a new beginning.'"

"After all this time together?" Jon asked. "That makes no sense."

Bryan shrugged and took another drag of his cigarette.

"Are you sure you don't want to smoke this instead?" Jason asked with a short laugh.

Bryan shook his head. "I don't need to be any more in my head than I already am."

"Well, I'm sorry, guy," Jason said and patted Bryan on the shoulder. "She'll realize she made a mistake. Geez. Maybe we did scare her away."

Bryan shook his head. "No. She told me she had fun at Saquish. She liked you guys."

"I wonder if Alyssa knows anything about it. Her brother dates Courtney's sister," Jon said.

"Oh, really?" Jason asked.

Bryan nodded. "Yeah, they've been together on and off for years, but Courtney and Alyssa have never met."

"Small world," Jason commented, trying to think of any reason why Courtney would break up with his friend so suddenly. Nothing came to him. "Hey, Cathy!" he called a moment later.

"What's up?" she called back to him and waved. She was floating around the pool in a string bikini—the most naked Jason had ever seen her. Her body was perfectly proportioned, and he wanted her more than he'd ever wanted anything.

"Do you want to hit this?" he asked, raising his bowl up in the air.

"No, I'm good!" she responded and waved him off.

He wondered if that meant she had taken Xanax or if she was too comfortable to climb out of the raft. As much as he loved her, he was worried about her. He could see her personality was changing. In the last few months, she had gone from agonizing over nearly every detail to not having much of a stance on anything. For that reason, Jason did not even want to try to sleep with her. It took every ounce of restraint within himself, but he knew the carefree person floating around his pool was not the girl he had fallen in love with. The girl in the pool was a product of the drugs Luke had been giving her for months. Although he knew his brother meant well, Jason wished he had never connected Cathy with Luke.

"I do!" Lisa cried and came running over to Jason, followed by Jeff.

"Sartelli, can I have a haul off that?" Jeff asked, motioning toward Bryan's cigarette.

"Have the rest," Bryan replied and passed it to him.

"What are you doing?!" Lisa cried out in protest. "You don't smoke!"

"Relax, pothead," Jeff said and placed his hand on her shoulder. "You don't have a leg to stand on."

Jason liked Jeff because he called Lisa out on her crap. Being extremely clean-cut and athletic—with a knack for pressing Lisa's buttons—Jeff was likely playing a prank on her. Jason highly doubted Jeff had any intention of smoking.

"You should just smoke weed," Lisa said while handing the bowl back to Jason. "It's better for you."

"I like having a clear head. I'll smoke weed the day I see you smoke a cigarette," Jeff retorted.

"That's it? That's all I have to do?" she asked before grabbing the cigarette out of his hand. "I'll smoke if you want me to."

Jeff rolled his eyes and reached to take it back from her. "Of course I don't want you to."

"Called your bluff!" Lisa cried happily. Then instead of handing the cigarette back to him, she took a drag of it. "Ugh. That's harsh!" she cried and threw it to the ground.

Jason dropped his jaw. He never expected to see her do that. She had given Chris more crap for smoking than Jason even had.

Jeff widened his eyes. "Why did you do that? I was kidding!"

Lisa laughed. "I figured, but now you owe me," she said in a mischievous tone.

"Oh, you *are* high," Jeff sang and gave her a playful glare before picking her up and throwing her in the pool.

Jason, Bryan, and Jon all laughed.

"You know how to handle her," Jason commented when Jeff walked back over to them.

"Lisa? I've been learning how to handle her for years," Jeff said. "Too many years."

"So, wait. Can we get back to the issue here?" Jason asked and tapped Bryan on the shoulder. "What do you think happened?"

"Dude, I literally don't know," Bryan replied and widened his eyes. "I was completely blindsided. She said I did nothing wrong."

"That's weird. She meets us and then breaks up with you a few days later?" Jason questioned him.

Bryan shrugged. "I wish I had an explanation for you."

"Did you and Courtney break up?" Jeff asked. Jeff had attended Hamilton Middle School with Courtney and Bryan, so he had seen them together regularly.

Bryan nodded. "She broke up with me over the phone last night—not even in person."

"That's weak," Jeff stated.

Jason agreed. It sounded to him like Courtney had something to hide.

Chapter 28

"Jon and I almost had sex last night," Alyssa said to Cathy as they floated around Jason's pool.

"What? No way!" Cathy cried, completely shocked to hear those words come out of her friend's mouth.

"Almost—I stopped him."

"What about his virginity pact?" Cathy asked and widened her eyes.

Alyssa laughed. "He hasn't mentioned that lately."

"Wow. You guys are moving fast!"

"We've known each other for more than half of our lives. That's not very fast when you think about it."

"Yeah, but you've been dating for less time than me and Jason. Jason's never even seen me naked."

"*That* is a miracle; he's the horniest kid I know."

"I told him about my virginity pact. Unlike you, he takes it seriously," Cathy said and nudged Alyssa playfully.

"I can't believe you whipped Jason Davids. I never thought that was possible."

Cathy laughed. "That's because I'm even better at reading people than he is," she said. "He thinks he's so rational and witty—and he is—but that's a small part of who he is. He doesn't even realize he wears his heart on his sleeve."

"Play nice with him," Alyssa warned and slapped Cathy's hand.

"Always," Cathy said and smiled at her friend. "Did you ever notice how all the guys listen to Jay? Even Chris, who I used to think was the leader of the group?"

Alyssa cocked her head to the side in thought. "Yeah, I guess you're right. Jay just always has good ideas."

Cathy nodded. "Did you ever notice anything else?"

"I've noticed a lot. What did you have in mind?" Alyssa questioned her.

"That he always listens to me," Cathy replied and glanced at her boyfriend.

Chapter 29

That afternoon, Chris sat in his bedroom, debating with himself over whether or not he should go to Jason's house. Jay had informed him that Lisa would be there with the boy she had been hooking up with. The news made a day by the pool with all of his best friends sound much less appealing. While he wanted to spend time with everyone, he knew he needed to give Lisa space. He also knew that seeing her with someone else would bother him deeply. They had been broken up for two and a half months, and each day he missed her more and more.

Although he had been using his longing for Lisa as motivation to abstain from taking pills, he had not cut Luke out of his life. He couldn't do so without making Marc suspicious. However, Luke had stopped offering Chris pills since his incident in April. Although Chris had tripped on mushrooms a few times and continued smoking weed, he felt like he was on a better path than he had been in the spring.

Sitting down at his computer, Chris logged onto Facebook to see if anyone had posted anything from Jason's house. Tagged in a post by Alyssa was a picture of her, Lisa, and Cathy, sitting on a large raft in the pool. The caption read: "Perfect day with my best ladies!" Lisa looked beautiful in a bikini, and Chris knew seeing her in person would certainly mess with his head. After tearing his eyes off the picture, he continued to scroll through his news feed. After a few minutes, he noticed he had a friend request from Courtney. He accepted the request and clicked on her profile. He was a bit surprised she had friend requested him. He assumed he had offended her at Saquish by asking if she wanted to get high. Her response had stuck with him for days. He admired her conviction and honestly wished he had more of it himself.

A couple minutes later, a private message popped up from Courtney, and Chris wondered if she was online at Jason's house or if Bryan had gone without her.

Courtney: Hey Chris! How are you?

Chris: Hi Courtney… good… how are you?

Courtney: I've been better.

Chris: What's wrong?

Courtney: Bryan and I broke up last night.

Chris: What? Why?

Courtney: It's complicated.

Chris: Okay. You don't have to explain yourself.

Courtney: I feel really bad, but Bryan told me for the past 2 years that I would not like hanging out with you guys. He said you were all into trouble. When I met you, I realized how stifled I felt by him. It made me question if I wanted to start high school attached to someone so controlling.

Chris: Geez. He must be devastated. Bryan isn't controlling. He was just afraid we would scare you away.

Courtney: I just need to be able to use my own judgement and decide who I want to hang out with. I know he was just trying to protect me.

Chris: Yeah… trust me when I say there's plenty he protected you from. Our group has been through a lot of drama in the past two years.

Courtney: Well, I'm glad I got to meet you guys finally.

Chris: Did you have fun on the 4th?

Courtney: So much fun!!

Chris: I'm sorry if I offended you by asking if you wanted to smoke weed. I wasn't thinking straight when I did that. Bryan told us you were straightedge. I should have known better. I hope I didn't make you feel uncomfortable.

Courtney: No not at all. Don't worry about that. He prepared me to meet all of you. I knew what to expect.

Chris: Okay

Courtney: Honestly, you guys were nicer than I expected.

Chris: Glad to hear

Courtney: What are you doing today?

Chris: Debating over whether I want to go to Jay's pool or not. My ex-girlfriend is there with another guy, and I think it would be awkward… but everyone is there, so if I don't go, it will be a waste of a wicked nice day.

Courtney: Do you like ice cream?

Chris: LOL yes… why?

Courtney: If you want to get your mind off your ex-girlfriend for a bit, you could help me get my mind off Bryan. We could meet up for ice cream in the center.

Chris cocked his head to the side as he re-read Courtney's last message. *She wants to hang out with me?* He was shocked, and he didn't know how to respond. He thought hanging out with her would be a great way to distract himself, but he feared doing so would upset Bryan.

Chris: I would love to meet up with you… I'm just a little worried about Bryan getting upset.

Courtney: It's totally up to you. He can't be that upset if he didn't tell you we broke up.

Chris dwelled on her comment. *Well, that's just Bryan. He's super private,* he thought. Truthfully, Chris liked the idea of spending time with Courtney. When he first saw her sitting with Bryan at the bonfire, his body had a strange reaction. He felt a strong urge to go talk to her for a reason he could not understand. From across the fire, she hadn't even looked pretty to him, so he knew it had nothing to do with her physical appearance. However, when he saw her up close, he realized she was as beautiful as Bryan had described. Chris was used to seeing girls all dolled up with makeup, fancy clothes, and high heels. Courtney had worn no makeup at all; her hair had been in a loose ponytail for much of the night; and she had worn modest clothing. However, there was something about her that Chris found extremely alluring. Their interactions on the Fourth of July had crossed his mind a few times over the last couple of days. Although he had been looking forward to seeing her again, he hadn't expected her to reach out to him. He tried but failed to figure out why he had found her so captivating.

Chris: I'm sure he's upset. He's just not open about personal stuff like that.

Courtney: It bothers me that I hurt him, but I need space. When I saw you were online, I figured you might be free to hang out.

Chris: Well yeah I'm free… I guess we could meet up. Were you thinking DQ or Scoops?

Courtney: Scoops! I want hard ice cream—half coffee half M&M in a sugar cone to be exact!

Chris: LOL. Okay. When do you want me to meet you there?

Courtney: I'll ask my sister to give me a ride. Do you have a cell phone?

Chris: No, I don't. I got one for my birthday, but it got taken away. My parents haven't been very happy with me lately.

Courtney: That's okay. I don't have one either. What's your number? I can call your house after I ask my sister.

Chris: Okay. Cool. 555-0635.

Courtney: Great. Thanks. Talk to you soon!

Chris: Sounds good.

This is so bizarre, he thought as he closed out of Facebook. *I was sure I had horrified this girl. Now I'm going to get ice cream with her?* He found the whole situation strange. Even so, he was excited to see her again. The best way he could describe Courtney was "a breath of fresh air." She was vibrant and cheerful with an attractive innocence. Stylistically, she appeared as different from Lisa as any girl could, but he thought, perhaps, that could be a good thing.

A moment later, the cordless phone on his nightstand began ringing, so he reached over to answer it. "Hello?" he called.

"Hey, it's me," replied Jason. "Are you coming over, guy?"

"Hey. No, I can't. I can't see Lisa. It will mess with my head."

"Oh, okay. Well, I'm going to get the firepit going later. Want me to call you if Lisa and Jeff leave?"

"Yeah, sounds good."

"Sorry, buddy. I wish you were here. Don't get bored and do anything crazy."

Chris laughed. "My only plan is to get ice cream downtown."

"All right, well, I'll call you later. Feel free to stop by if you change your mind."

"Will do," Chris responded and then ended the call. Within seconds, his telephone began ringing again.

"Hi, is Chris there?" a female voice asked.

"That's me," Chris replied.

"Hey, it's Court. My sister said we can leave in twenty minutes. Do you want to meet me there in, like, a half hour?"

"Yeah, sure. It's only a ten-minute walk from my house. I'll meet you by the big rock."

"Okay! Sounds great!" Courtney cried. "See you soon!"

"All right, bye," Chris said before hanging up the phone. *She sounds excited to see me*, he thought.

While getting ready to head to Scoops, Chris realized that getting closer with Courtney could encourage him to get sober. Despite the strides he had made since the spring, the fact that he had either smoked weed or drank alcohol every day over the last couple of months bothered him. He needed all the straightedge friends he could get. As "the life of the party," he tended to bring out the wild side in everyone, but that was something he wanted to change.

Chapter 30

When Courtney arrived at the ice cream shop, Chris was surprised to see her get out of a BMW with not only her sister, but also Alyssa's brother John.

"Hi!" Courtney cried as she spotted Chris standing by the large rock with an American flag painted on it.

Chris smiled as she jogged over to him. John and Courtney's sister glanced at him quickly and then headed over to the window to get in line. "What's up?" he greeted Courtney as she approached him.

"It's good to see you," Courtney said and leaned forward to hug him. He thought her countenance appeared bright.

"You too," Chris responded and hugged her back. "Does your sister date John Kelly?"

Courtney nodded. "They've been together on and off since seventh grade. How do you know John?"

"He's my friend's brother. They live a couple streets over from me, so I've known John for years."

"Oh, small world," Courtney said. "Actually, small Montgomery is what I should say," she added with a laugh. Just like at Saquish, she was dressed modestly and wearing no makeup. The sparkle in her sky-blue eyes caught his attention, and he believed makeup likely would have taken away from her beauty.

"Right," Chris agreed. "So, how are you holding up?" he asked and sat down on the rock.

Courtney sat down beside him and sighed. "I'm okay. I know it's for the best."

"What made you reach out to me today?"

"It probably seemed random, huh?" she questioned him.

Chris nodded and stared at her curiously.

"I'm just kind of drawn to you," she admitted. "I don't even mean that in a physical way; I just feel like we are meant to be in each other's lives."

Chris was taken aback by her candid response. His conscience would not allow him to admit that he was drawn to her, too. The last thing he wanted to do was hit on his friend's ex-girlfriend. "I'm shocked," he said. "Knowing what I know about you, I didn't think you'd have any interest in getting to know *me*."

"Why not?"

Chris laughed. "Because I have a terrible reputation!"

Courtney rolled her eyes. "I know I should care more about stuff like that because I want to get into politics like my dad someday, but honestly, your reputation doesn't bother me."

"Well, I've been trying to turn things around lately and make better decisions," Chris remarked.

"Who's your ex-girlfriend at Jay's house?" Courtney asked curiously.

"Lisa Ankerman. She went to Sterling."

"I don't know her. Why is she at your best friend's house instead of you?"

"She's best friends with Jay's girlfriend, and Jay let's Cathy run their lives," Chris replied.

Courtney laughed. "Well, that must be kind of awkward. Why did you break up?"

Chris took a deep breath. "I wasn't in a good place a few months ago. It took a toll on us."

"How long were you guys together?"

"Aren't we supposed to be getting our minds off our exes?" Chris asked with a short laugh.

Courtney giggled. "Yes! I'm sorry! I'm just super nosey."

"It's okay," Chris said. "Curiosity can be a good thing."

"So, forget about Lisa; tell me about you!"

"Me? What do you want to know about me?"

157

"I heard you're a really good athlete. Do you think you'll play football at MLH?"

"Oh, definitely," Chris replied. "The JV coach already contacted me and said he wants to fit me on his roster. They don't usually let freshmen play for JV, so it would be a great opportunity. My cousin Marc is co-captain of varsity. We're a big football family."

"That's great!" Courtney exclaimed. "Do you like baseball?"

Chris nodded. "I play every spring."

"We should go to a Red Sox game sometime. We have season tickets!"

"Now, that would be fun."

"Are you saying ice cream isn't?"

Chris laughed and stood up from the rock. "Why don't we go get ice cream, and then I'll let you know."

Courtney smiled at him and stood up. "I didn't tell my sister I was coming here to meet you, so she might be surprised to see you."

"I'm sure John told her who I was when he saw me," Chris gathered while walking toward the line. "What's your sister's name?"

"Day."

"That's different."

"I know; I'm glad I was born second!"

Chris laughed. "Well, if she's dating John, then she's doing all right for herself. He's a super nice kid."

Courtney nodded. "He's a wicked good kid. He's the one who got my sister to start going to church, and then I saw how it changed her life, so I started going, too."

"That's good," Chris said. "I didn't realize John was religious. His sister isn't."

Courtney shrugged. "I don't know her."

"She's one of the 'horrible people' Bryan was trying to protect you from," Chris joked.

"Ah, gotcha."

They only had to wait in line for a couple of minutes before ordering their ice cream. Courtney offered to pay since it had been her idea. Chris figured he should let her so it wouldn't sound to Bryan like he had taken her on a date.

"Courtney! Come over here!" Day called out from a nearby picnic table.

"Okay!" Courtney responded. "Come meet my sister," she said and tugged on Chris's shirt.

Chris took a deep breath as he followed Courtney over to the picnic table. He imagined all of the horrible things that John might have told Day about him. John was good friends with Marc, so he knew *a lot* about Chris.

"Hi!" Courtney greeted John and Day. "This is my friend, Chris."

"I know Chris," John said with a smirk. "How do you guys know each other?"

"Bryan," Courtney replied immediately.

"Well, that makes sense," John commented.

"Hi, I'm Day," Courtney's sister introduced herself with a friendly smile. She looked a lot like Courtney, despite having much lighter hair.

"Nice to meet you," Chris replied.

"Court, we want to get back to the pool," Day said. "Are you ready to leave? We're not trying to cut your conversation short, but it's a wicked nice day."

"Chris, do you want to come over and hang out by my pool?" Courtney asked as she turned to him.

Chris widened his eyes. "Um, okay," he replied in a surprised tone.

"Great, then I'm ready to leave," Courtney said matter-of-factly.

Day and John looked at each other strangely, and Chris wondered if they knew Courtney had broken up with Bryan.

159

"Okay, sounds good," Day said with a shrug and then jumped off the picnic table. As Chris followed everyone to Day's car, he wondered what thoughts were going through their minds. John had never attended a party at Chris's house when Jordan or Taylor had been around, so at least he had never seen Chris drunk. However, Day looked familiar, which meant she had likely partied with his cousins.

"Why don't you text Marc, Michelle, Matt, Ally, and Katie and invite them over?" Day suggested to John after they climbed into her black three-series.

"Okay," John said and picked his phone up out of the cup holder. "I'll call Marc and Matt and see what they're up to."

"Whatever you do, don't invite Luke," Day said. "He's too much for me to handle lately."

"I hear ya," John said and brought his phone to his ear.

Chris found it strange that Courtney's sister's life was so entwined with his own friends and family. He had not expected to possibly end up hanging out with his cousin that day. Thinking about it, he realized that Marc would be happy to hear that Chris was spending time with Courtney, Day, and John.

"Hey, dude," John said into his phone. "Do you want to meet us at Day's pool? We'll be there in about ten minutes... Oh... okay... Nice! Are you with Matty? (pause) Oh, okay. I'll give him a call." John ended the call and then turned to Day. "Marc's heading into Boston to go to the Red Sox game with Taylor."

"How's Taylor doing?" Day asked.

"Marc isn't sure," John replied. "What do you think, Chris?"

Chris widened his eyes. He had a lot of thoughts on Taylor, but he did not want to horrify Courtney. "I think Marc's right to be worried about him," Chris responded.

"We haven't seen him since Christmas," Day said. "I think his injury really threw him off."

"Yeah," Chris agreed. "I'm glad Marc's going to see him. Jordan said he's going to try to spend some time with him this summer, too. I

160

think T's really depressed." The fact that they were conversing about his own family put Chris to ease. Even though he hardly knew Courtney or Day, it felt like they were all a part of the same circle.

"What's up, Matt?" John called into his phone a few seconds later. "You should come by Day's pool. We're heading there now… Okay… Ha, yeah… call Ally and tell her to invite Michelle and Katie. Okay, cool. See you in a bit." When John hung up the phone, he turned to Day and said, "Matt said Ally was heading to his house to lay out, but Jason took over the pool with his friends, so they'll head to your house once she gets there."

This is bizarre, Chris thought. *Courtney is literally surrounded by all the same older kids as me. How did our paths never cross before Saquish?* Then something dawned on him: Matt would likely tell Jason if he saw Chris at Courtney's. Marc wouldn't be there, so Jason would wonder how Chris had ended up there—meaning Chris was going to have a lot of explaining to do.

Chapter 31

After a fun-filled day by the Angelettis' pool, Matt offered Chris a ride home around seven o'clock. "Why weren't you at my house today?" he questioned Chris after they climbed into his SUV with Ally and Michelle.

"Lisa was there, so I decided to keep my distance," Chris replied from the backseat. Ally was riding shotgun, and Michelle was sitting to his right. It was strange for him to be in such close proximity to the girl who had divided Jordan and Marc. However, he knew that had never been Michelle's intent. She was the epitome of a good person.

"Lisa can be a pain in the ass," Matt commented with a short laugh. "She's been at my house a lot lately."

"I bet," Chris said flatly, hoping Matt would change the subject.

"How did you end up hanging out with Courtney today?" Ally asked while turning around to face Chris.

"Courtney messaged me on Facebook and asked if I wanted to get ice cream," Chris replied and locked his blue eyes on Ally.

Matt and Ally were likely to get voted "Class Couple" in the fall. Matt was the captain of the football team, and Ally was the captain of the cheerleading squad. Although it was extremely stereotypical for them to date, they were not stereotypical Montgomery teenagers. Chris had never once seen Matt or Ally drunk, and they both frowned upon drug use. In fact, they used their leadership positions in sports to encourage others not to use drugs. They were a part of a class in which "everyone" was friends. Even though they had a close-knit group, they were friendly with everyone else in their grade. Marc had always told Chris that he had the best class because there were no cliques. Chris imagined that his own grade was going to be quite cliquey. They weren't even in high school yet, and there were already groups that avoided each other. The senior class certainly gave the younger kids a reason to look up to them, and Matt Davids led the charge.

"I didn't realize you two were friends," Ally commented and cocked her head to the side. "Doesn't she date your friend?"

Chris shook his head. "They broke up."

Ally widened her eyes. "Oh. So, have you two been hanging out lately?"

"No. This was only our second time."

Ally smiled at him. "Courtney's awesome," she said. "You should keep hanging out with her."

"I'd like to," Chris admitted.

"Marc's going to be so happy to hear you were with us today," Michelle said. "He worries about you a lot."

Chris put his head down. "I'm sure he does," he said quietly, assuming everyone in the car knew a lot about his past.

"Should I be worried about Jason?" Matt asked. "I caught him smoking weed a few times this year."

"You should be worried about Luke," Chris stated flatly. "Jay just smokes weed to calm himself down from the Adderall your parents make him take."

"I can keep an eye on Luke because he hangs out with us a lot," Matt said, "but Jason is another story."

"Jay's fine. I think, anyway," Chris said, a bit surprised by Matt's concern.

"He gets bored too easily," Matt stated. "I can see him experimenting with a lot of different drugs, and after next year, I won't be in Montgomery to keep an eye on him. That bothers me."

"Jay's girlfriend is pretty tame," Chris said. "She keeps him in line."

"He got her so high last weekend that she had to sleep over our house!" Matt exclaimed.

"Oh, really?" Chris asked, surprised he had not heard that story.

"He swears they didn't have sex, but I think the two of them are going to ruin each other," Matt commented. "Jay was always super independent. I don't know how this girl got him tied down, but he doesn't do anything without her."

"They're good together," Chris assured him. "She's really smart, just like Jay, so they have similar interests."

"Her family goes to my church," Michelle spoke up. "I think she's a pretty good kid, Matt."

"I know my brother, and I know something's not right," Matt insisted. "I hope he gets his head on straight and doesn't corrupt Cathy any more than he already has."

"Trust me when I say you should be more worried about Luke than Jay," Chris pressed.

"Luke's been spending a ton of time with our friend Missy," Ally said. "I think they're going to start dating soon."

"Missy Kent?" Chris asked, thinking of the blonde bombshell who was friends with Marc.

"Yeah," Ally replied and rolled her eyes. "She's just as wild as him; they're a perfect storm."

"So, worry about them," Chris said. "Jay and Cathy are fine."

"No, they're not," Matt stated flatly. "You're just too close with them to see it."

Chapter 32

When Chris arrived home that night, he had three missed calls from Jason. Before calling him back, Chris made himself dinner and reflected on his day. It was one of the only times he had had fun while being sober in the last year. Spending time with Courtney had been refreshing, and Chris could understand why Bryan had distanced himself from their friends to be with her. Around eight o'clock, Chris called Jason's cell phone.

"Dude, I thought you were just going to get ice cream today," Jason said as soon as he answered the call.

"I did," Chris replied in a perplexed manner.

"Then why are you tagged on Ally's Instagram, sitting by a pool fancier than mine?"

"Oh, she posted a picture?"

"According to Facebook, Marc's at the Red Sox game with Taylor, so how did you end up with Matt and Ally?" Jason asked curiously.

"I ran into John Kelly and his girlfriend while I was getting ice cream," Chris replied. "Courtney was with them, and they invited me back to the Angelettis' pool."

"What?!" Jason exclaimed. "Dude, Courtney broke up with Bryan last night. Did you know that?"

"Yeah, I heard."

"Well, why did she invite you to her house?"

"I don't know."

"Bryan's a mess! He left here about an hour ago. He's heartbroken, guy. You can't hang out with his ex."

"You hang out with my ex all the time," Chris retorted. "I don't hold it against you."

Jason sighed. "You have a point, but Bryan's not going to see it that way."

"She said she broke up with him because he was trying to shelter her. She didn't like that he kept her from being friends with us."

"It sounds like she explained herself a lot better to you than to Bryan. He has no idea why she broke up with him."

"I don't know what to tell you, Jay. I had a great day with a bunch of good people. I need more of that in my life. I would have been at your house if Lisa wasn't there."

"Lisa and Jeff are still here," Jason informed him, "or else I would tell you to come over."

"It's fine. I'm good. I'm tired from being in the sun all day."

"Who was at Courtney's?"

"John Kelly, Courtney's sister, Matt, Ally, Katie McKnight, and Michelle Taylor."

"Are you going to tell Bryan?"

"I don't know."

"He's not on Instagram, so he's not going to see Ally's post, but you should tell him anyway."

"Wouldn't that be like rubbing salt in a wound?"

Jason sighed. "Maybe? I don't know. I never expected her to want to hang out with *you*."

"Right? Me either."

"I'm going to stay out of this," Jason declared. "I can sense drama on the radar, and I don't want any part of it."

"Dude, it's not like we hooked up," Chris stated defensively.

"Why do you want to hang out with her?"

"She's the type of person I need to be around right now. I can't constantly surround myself with people who do drugs if I want to stay clean."

"I don't know Courtney, but spending time with Matt's friends will definitely help you stay away from pills."

"Matt's worried about you."

"Oh. That's just because he found out I smoke weed," Jason said carelessly.

"I told him he should worry more about Luke than you."

"Good!" Jason cried. "He should!"

"You should talk to Matt and let him know you're okay," Chris suggested. "You are, right?"

"I'm fine," Jason asserted. "He's just freaked out about the weed."

"Is there any way he knows about the other stuff?"

"No. No way."

"Well, he's more worried about you than Luke."

"That's just because he likes me better than Luke," Jason retorted with a laugh.

"He said you got Cathy so baked that she had to sleep over your house last weekend. Is that true?"

"Yeah. I didn't tell you because we hung out with Jeff and Lisa that night. I try not to mention Lisa to you," Jason replied.

"Oh. Okay. Well, he's upset that you got her high. He thinks you're corrupting her."

"Luke is corrupting her," Jason stated flatly. "I'm trying to figure out how to undo what Luke has done."

Chris sighed. "Why don't you tell Matt that Luke's dealing drugs? He'll set him straight and make him stop giving pills to Cathy."

"I don't know what would happen if she stopped taking Xanax," Jason admitted. "She might go nuts. She's been riding a Xanax high for almost three months."

"Well, even I know that's not good," Chris said. "She doesn't drink, right?"

"Right. Thank God. She used to not drink because of her religious beliefs, but I doubt she even cares about them anymore. She doesn't seem to care about anything lately. I told her Luke made me drink at Saquish, and she laughed."

"Geez. That doesn't sound anything like the Cathy I know and love," Chris commented, growing concerned about her. "You should ask Luke to stop supplying her with pills."

"Dude, I'm really afraid she'll go crazy without them," Jason whispered.

"It sounds like she's going crazy with them," Chris stated matter-of-factly.

Jason sighed. "Let's talk about this later. I can only hide in the bathroom for so long. Cathy, Lisa, Jeff, and Luke are all in the kitchen."

"All right, guy. I'll talk to you tomorrow," Chris said before ending the call.

The fact that Chris had taken Xanax on about ten different occasions did not subdue his concern for Cathy. If she had been taking it every day for a few months, then she was likely addicted to it. He remembered Lisa telling him that Cathy did not want to go on anxiety medication because she did not want to become an emotional zombie. *I wonder what changed her mind?* He wanted to figure out a way to help her, but the only thing he could think of doing was outing Luke to Matt. Jason's need for harmony made him conflict averse, so Chris was not surprised that he did not want to start a feud between his brothers. *But wouldn't a feud be worth it if it saved Cathy from a prescription drug habit?*

When Chris tried to fall asleep that night, he could not get Cathy off his mind. She was kind, smart, beautiful, and a gifted athlete. She had strong morals and a good head on her shoulders. She was one of the last people Chris would expect to get into benzos. He knew her situation was likely eating away at Jason, which could explain why he had been so eager to trip lately, as well as why he had started snorting Adderall. Chris regretted ever convincing Jason to snort it with him. Previously, Jason had no idea that snorting it would get him high. He had a cache of the pills he had not taken in seventh grade, so his supply seemed limitless. With Jason abusing Adderall and Cathy taking Xanax, they were likely headed for turmoil.

168

Chris tossed and turned all night, feeling incredibly angry with himself for getting his friends into drugs. *I introduced Jon to alcohol and weed, which ruined his relationship with Chantal; I got Bryan to try alcohol, cigarettes, weed, and mushrooms, which could have messed up his relationship with Courtney if he had actually liked drugs; I introduced Lisa to weed and molly; I got Jason into mushrooms, weed, mescaline, acid, and snorting things—I am a horrible person.* Thankfully, Chris's conscience had not allowed him to introduce his friends to benzos or painkillers. However, Luke had plenty of Vicodin, Xanax, Klonopin, and Percocet to go around, so all of Chris's friends were at risk for getting deeper into drugs.

Guilt surmounted Chris whenever he was sober, but it was something he was learning to address. Earlier that day, he admitted to Courtney that he felt bad for introducing his friends to drugs, and she suggested he use that for motivation to get sober. He felt comfortable confiding in her. Despite her strong religious views, she had not been judgmental. She seemed genuinely interested in learning more about him.

Spending the day with Courtney had tremendously lifted his spirits, and he hoped she would reach out to him again soon. He did not know if he could keep his developing friendship with her a secret from Bryan. Hiding something from one of his best friends was not in his character, and if he did, it would only be to avoid hurting Bryan. However, he knew Bryan would find out in the long run and likely feel betrayed if he did not hear about it first from Chris.

Chapter 33

Five days later, Jason was floating on a large raft in his pool with Cathy. He had purposely not invited anyone else over that day because there were a lot of things he needed to discuss with her.

"So, this weekend, I want to spend some time with Chris," Jason began while taking hold of Cathy's hand. "He hasn't been able to hang out with us lately because Lisa has been around, and I don't want him to think I'm choosing her over him."

"You're the one who said he wouldn't care if we hung out with Lisa and Jeff," Cathy responded and turned toward him with a perplexed expression on her face.

"Right, and he doesn't care, but he still needs to spend time with us," Jason said. "The last thing he needs while trying to stay away from pills is for his friends to ditch him."

Cathy sat up to face him. "So, we should split up our time between Lisa and Chris, just like Chris split up his time between you and Jon when we hated him."

Jason laughed. "*We* never hated Jon; *you* hated him."

"I still kind of do," Cathy admitted.

"So, are you okay with leaving Lisa and Jeff out of our plans this weekend so Chris can hang out?" Jason asked.

"Of course," Cathy replied and lay back down on the raft. "What has he been up to lately? I haven't seen him in weeks."

"He's actually been doing okay. He's been spending more time with Marc's friends, and I think they're good influences on him."

"Good."

"But there's someone else he's been hanging out with, and we need to talk about that."

Cathy again sat up and looked at Jason. "Is he dating someone?"

"No," Jason replied. "He's not over Lisa."

170

Cathy shrugged. "It keeps me from having panic attacks. It keeps me from being sad about Chantal. It's worth it to me."

"But it's making you cold."

"Me?! You're the one who wants to hang out with the girl who just broke Bryan's heart! I'm the one who feels bad for him!" Cathy cried defensively.

"Did you take Xanax today?" Jason asked.

"No. Floating around your pool doesn't give me anxiety."

"So, you don't take it every day?"

"No. I take it before school, church, and social events, so that equates to most days but not every day."

"And you don't go through withdrawal without it?"

"No," Cathy said flatly.

"How much do you take when you take it?" Jason asked, realizing he should have inquired about that a long time ago.

"The pills are only a half of a milligram. I've taken more than one in a day, but I don't do that often."

"Okay. So, you're not physically addicted to it yet. You should stop taking it while you still can," Jason stated in a serious tone. "I read up on Xanax addiction, and it is not fun. People can even die from withdrawal. It's a very scary drug, and I wish I never told you to try it."

"That's why I don't want to be prescribed it. I read up on it, too, and the idea of being dependent on it scares me. People can go through withdrawal for over ten years."

Jason was extremely relieved to learn that Cathy had not developed a physical dependence on the drug; however, he wanted her to stop taking it as soon as possible. "You're completely sober right now. That's why you feel bad for Bryan and why you don't want to hang out with Courtney," he reasoned. "When you're on drugs, you're different."

"Well, when you're on drugs, you're different, too."

"How so?"

Cathy cocked her head to the side before bluntly stating, "You're less fun when you're baked, and when you trip, I can't stand you."

Jason widened his eyes. "That's why I don't trip around you anymore," he responded defensively.

"You smoke weed every day. It chills you out too much. It takes away the sparkle in your eye I was always so attracted to."

Jason was a bit taken back by her statement. "Are you not attracted to me anymore?"

Cathy rolled her eyes. "Of course I am. I'm just saying you're more attractive when you're sober."

"I like you better sober, too," Jason admitted and raised his eyebrows at her.

"So, what do you want me to do?" Cathy questioned him. "Live with panic attacks and crippling anxiety? Walk around depressed all the time?"

"No. I don't want you to suffer, but now that I've seen the way Xanax affects you, I regret ever giving it to you. You once told me you didn't want to become an emotional zombie. You were right; when you're on Xanax, you're emotionally unavailable."

Cathy looked as though she was about to cry, and Jason feared he may have been a bit too frank with her. The last thing he wanted to do was give her an anxiety attack. Jason sat up on the raft and pulled her down on top of him so that her back was against his stomach. "I'm sorry," he said and wrapped his arms around her tightly. "I'm just worried about you."

"I'm worried about you, too," she said in a faint voice. "You must be addicted to Adderall by now. You take it every day."

Jason sighed. "I can wean myself off of it if it will make you feel better."

"Really?" Cathy asked in a surprised tone. "I don't want you to mess up your grades. I know you have work to do over the summer for your AP classes."

"It's nothing I can't handle without Adderall."

176

"You would stop taking it for me?"

"I would do anything to make you happy," Jason replied.

"Be honest with me. Have you ever snorted it?" Cathy asked.

Jason could feel the color drain from his face. "Why would you ask me that?"

"Because Lisa told me Chris used to snort it to get high," she replied, "and I assumed he got it from you."

Jason took a deep breath. "I've snorted it with Chris a few times," he admitted.

"I figured," Cathy said sadly. "You didn't tell me because you were afraid I would worry about you?"

"Yup."

"So, you would stop doing it if I asked you to?"

"Yup."

"I can't ask you to stop taking medicine you're prescribed. To be honest, I don't mind the effect it has on you. I like it when you're driven and excited. I don't like it when you're stoned."

"I'm naturally driven and excited," Jason said. "All Adderall does is intensify that part of my personality. I think it's messing up my sleep schedule. I hardly sleep at night; then I just depend on Adderall for energy when I get up in the morning."

"You sound like you don't want to take it anymore."

"I'm actually really confused about it," Jason admitted. "I can't tell if it helps me or hurts me. I think I only like weed because it brings me down from the Adderall high."

"Why don't you cut out weed *and* Adderall for a while and see how you feel?" Cathy suggested.

"Yeah. I'll try do to that this summer. Coming off Adderall isn't easy."

"You've done it before; you can do it again," Cathy assumed. "We're both wicked messed up, aren't we?"

Jason laughed. "A little bit."

"Who knows?"

"Chris… Luke… No one else on my end."

"Lisa knows, so Jeff probably does, too."

"Neither one of them has a big mouth. They won't let rumors get around. We know stuff about them, too."

"Lisa would get kicked off cheerleading for smoking pot," Cathy said. "We don't really have anything on Jeff. He's kind of perfect."

"He loves Lisa," Jason stated. "That's enough to keep him quiet."

"I feel bad for him. Lisa's too afraid to love him back. I think she's using him for comfort and physical pleasure."

Jason laughed. "I know a lot of guys who wouldn't mind Lisa using them for physical pleasure."

Cathy slapped Jason lightly on the leg. "You know what I mean."

"I do, but don't worry about Jeff. Lisa will commit to him in due time, unless Chris suddenly gets better and sweeps her off her feet."

"I think he would have to be clean for a long time before she would give him another chance," Cathy reasoned.

"Well, by then she'll probably have feelings for Jeff," Jason predicted, "so I doubt they'll end up back together."

"If she sleeps with Jeff, then we'll know for sure that she doesn't love him."

Jason laughed. "What?"

"She told me she liked Chris too much to have sex with him," Cathy replied. "She said her brothers taught her that sex complicates things."

"Interesting. Most people view sex as an expression of love."

"Well, did you love the two girls you slept with?"

Jason could feel his face turning red. "No."

"Right. Exactly."

Chapter 34

***

8 Months Later – March of 2018 (Present Day)

Taylor was walking across Northeastern's campus with his head down, hoping no one would recognize him, but nevertheless being bombarded by students who were excited to see him back at school. "I was only here for a meeting," he stated over and over again while trying to make his way back to his Jeep. Despite how popular everyone was making him feel, he felt like a failure who should have been well on his way to graduation—not discussing his transfer options.

"Taylor?" a female voice called out, stealing him away from his condemning thoughts.

He turned to his left only to see Marc's friends, Katie McKnight and Michelle Taylor, walking toward him. He lowered his eyebrows, wondering why they were at Northeastern. He had not seen either girl in over a year.

"How are you?!" Michelle cried out as she threw her arms around him in a tight embrace.

He hugged her back, finding it bizarre that he had already seen four of Marc's friends that afternoon. "Good," he replied.

When Michelle let go of him, Katie was right beside her with a hug in waiting. "It's good to see you," Katie said. "Are you back here?"

"No. I wish," Taylor replied, glancing back and forth between the two girls. He could not believe how grown up they looked. He had known them since they first became close with Marc in middle school. Realizing they would be going off to college in six months made him feel old. "I just had a meeting with my old advisor about something. What are you girls doing in Boston?"

"This," Michelle replied with a wide grin. "Touring colleges."

"Ah, that makes sense. Did you both apply here?" Taylor asked.

Michelle and Katie nodded.

"Co-op has made this school so popular. I don't know if I would have gotten in without football," Taylor remarked.

"Well, the nursing school might be my first choice, but Michelle has her heart set on Notre Dame," Katie informed him.

Taylor widened his eyes, startled to hear the name of the university he had once planned to attend. As he glanced at Michelle, he wondered why she would consider going to school with Jordan. According to Marc, Jordan had tried to date-rape Michelle at a party two and a half years prior; according to Jordan, he had never laid a hand on her. Although Taylor broke up the fight between his brothers that night, he never learned the truth of what had made Michelle so sick. If Michelle was willing to attend college with Jordan, then he most likely had not drugged her.

Michelle smiled. "I have a friend on the football team who speaks rather highly of the school," she said in a lighthearted manner.

Taylor raised his eyebrows. "Jordan?" he asked.

Michelle smiled again. "He's flying home tonight to spend Easter with your family. He passed up on a trip to Punta Cana for you guys."

Taylor cocked his head to the side. "Since when do you talk to Jordan?"

"Since he came home for Christmas," Michelle replied with a sparkle in her eye.

Taylor grinned, feeling a great sense of relief and knowing for sure that his brother had not tried to force himself onto Michelle. "That's great," he said. "I had no idea Jordan was coming home."

"Oops. Sorry if it was supposed to be a surprise," Michelle apologized with a cringe. "He probably never thought I would run into you in a million years."

"It *is* strange," Taylor commented. "I haven't been on this campus in months."

"Eerie," Katie said and shuddered.

"Well, there's no school tomorrow, so a bunch of our friends are going out tonight in the Seaport," Michelle explained. "Katie and I headed in early to visit BU and here. Actually, Marc's in town, too. He has a meeting at BC."

That makes a lot of sense, Taylor thought, assuming that was why Luke and Cathy had been in the city. "Tell him to visit me," Taylor said. "I miss him."

Michelle nodded. "I will. He'll be shocked that we saw you."

"Does he know you've been talking to Jordan?" Taylor questioned her curiously.

Michelle dropped her brown eyes and shook her head. "No, not yet."

"He thinks Jordan drugged you," Taylor said in a low tone. "You need to set him straight."

Michelle looked up at Taylor. "I told him Jordan never touched me that night."

"He thinks that's only because he and Chris barged into the room before he could," Taylor whispered and looked her directly in the eye. She looked sincere but confused.

"I got sick, and Jordan tried to take care of me," Michelle stated. "He didn't drug me."

Taylor glanced back and forth from Michelle to Katie, observing that both girls looked uncomfortable. He wondered if Michelle even knew that Marc and Jordan were in a feud. Marc could have very well kept that to himself. He was a far more private person than Taylor or Jordan. *Jordan must have told her*, Taylor reasoned. *Jordan holds nothing back.* "Do you realize that Marc and Jordan haven't gotten along since that party?"

"That's part of the reason why Jordan's coming home," she replied. "He wants to make things right with Marc."

"I don't think talking to you is going to better his chances with Marc," Taylor said matter-of-factly. "I'm pretty sure Marc still has feelings for you."

Michelle rolled her eyes. "Marc has a new girlfriend," she said. "That's the only reason why I felt comfortable letting Jordan back into my life. Marc hooked up with a freshman in December, and he brought her to my ski house over Christmas break. They're still together."

"So, you stopped talking to Jordan a couple years ago because of Marc?" Taylor questioned her.

Michelle nodded. "Marc is my best friend, and I saw how much it bothered him to see me with Jordan."

"He thinks you stopped talking to Jordan because Jordan drugged you," Taylor reiterated. "You need to tell him the truth."

Michelle and Katie both winced.

Taylor looked at them in a perplexed manner. "Why does it seem like you don't want to do that?"

Michelle sighed and glanced from Katie to Taylor. "*Jordan* didn't put anything in my drink that night," she stated with emphasis and eyed Taylor expectantly.

He squinted in thought, thinking back to the party, trying to remember what drugs had been circulating around that time. Molly? Liquid G? Coke? Michelle was clearly trying to tell him something.

"We should get going," Katie said and latched onto Michelle's arm while eyeing Taylor precariously. "The library closes at five today, and I really want to see it."

At that moment, Taylor realized Michelle was the only person who could fix Marc and Jordan's relationship. Hopefully she cared enough about both of them to tell Marc the truth. While Taylor was certain Michelle had not wittingly taken any drugs, it sounded to him like something had, in fact, been put in her drink—by *someone*. Why Michelle or Katie would feel the need to protect that person's identity was beyond puzzling.

"Okay," Michelle agreed. "It was so good to see you, Taylor!" she cried and threw her arms around him again. "I'm going to fix this," she whispered into his ear.

Chapter 35

At four-thirty, Marc was still sitting in his truck with Luke and Cathy in one of BC's parking lots, hoping that Taylor would call him back. He had no idea what neighborhood Taylor lived in, or he would have headed in that direction. He did not want to ask his parents for Taylor's new address because they would make a big deal about Marc going to see him. He sighed. "He's probably asleep. I wish I knew where he lived."

"What did you find out, dude?" Luke asked. "Why do you want to see him so badly?"

"I can't tell you," Marc replied.

"Is T in trouble?" Luke questioned him.

Marc began to wonder if Luke knew where Taylor lived. *How can I ask him without giving away that I know Taylor is his dealer?* Marc had opted to not confront Luke about selling drugs to Chris, Cathy, or Jason because Luke had a big mouth, and Marc did not want people in Montgomery finding out that Taylor was a drug dealer. After much consideration in November, Marc had decided to address the problem in a different way: keeping Cathy and Jason away from each other. He reasoned that would allow Chris time to help Jason get sober while he helped Cathy. The molly and coke that Luke had been sporadically doing did not concern Marc as much as the benzos and opiates Cathy and Jason had been using. Since November, Marc had been trying his hardest to undo the damage Taylor and Luke had caused.

"Is he?" Luke repeated, pulling Marc away from his thoughts.

"No. I just need to see him," Marc responded.

"Well, why don't we head to dinner somewhere and wait for his call?" Luke suggested. "You must be hungry. Did they feed you in your meeting?"

"I wish I knew what direction to head in," Marc commented. "Where do you think we should go, Luke?" he asked flatly, hoping his friend would point him in the right direction.

Cathy sent Marc a strange look, and he realized she appeared more anxious than usual.

"Let's go to Maggiano's!" Luke suggested brightly. "Katie and Michelle are close by, and Missy is on her way into the city with Pat and Laurelle. We can have a family-style dinner."

How cozy, Marc thought. It made sense to head towards the theatre district, as it was close to Northeastern, where Katie and Michelle were touring. He assumed Taylor still lived somewhere nearby because his brother was a creature of habit and liked what was familiar. "Good idea," Marc replied. "Are you okay with Italian, Cathy?"

Cathy nodded.

"Are you okay in general?" Marc questioned her.

She nodded again but failed to make eye contact with him.

"So, what did you guys do today?" he asked while pulling out of the parking lot.

"We had lunch in South Boston and then went to the Bruins Pro Shop," Luke replied immediately. "You two should go to the game tonight while the rest of us go out in the Seaport. I bought Cathy a new Bruins hat. She's ready."

Marc raised his eyebrows, not hating the idea. Because Cathy was only fifteen, she could not get into the club his friends were planning to go to. "Do you want to go to the game tonight?" he asked without taking his eyes off the road.

"I love hockey," Cathy replied. "I just don't have money on me for a ticket or for dinner. Sorry, I planned on going to class, not coming into Boston."

"My money's your money," Luke said. "I'll buy you dinner; Marc can take you to the game."

"I'll get us tickets if it's okay with your parents," Marc offered.

"I called my mom when we were on our way back to BC," Cathy informed him. "I told her I was going to pick you up with Luke, and she said I could stay out 'til eleven."

"My God," Marc remarked. "You did that without even lying."

"CK's no fool," Luke stated and patted Cathy on the shoulder. "My brother trained her well."

Preview of Gripped Part 3
Chapter 1

March of 2018

After walking across Northeastern's snow-covered campus and being bombarded by people seeming happy to see him, Taylor Dunkin reached his black Jeep Grand Cherokee. He climbed inside and started the engine, planning to gather his thoughts before driving home. He had to process not only what his former advisor had said, but also the news from Michelle Taylor.

Upon review of his transcript, Taylor had learned that he had seventy-two out of ninety credits that were transfer eligible. However, his cumulative GPA was below the desired 3.0 and barely above the minimum 2.5 required to transfer at most institutions. Although he could write an essay describing how his injury had affected his performance in the classroom, without football, his chance of being admitted to a college as highly ranked as Northeastern was unlikely. He sat in amazement of how one year of bad choices could mess up a lifetime's worth of hard work. He had graduated in the top ten percent of his class and had scored in the ninety-seventh percentile on the SAT. Thankfully his SAT score was still applicable, but his GPA was shameful in his eyes.

His former advisor, Mr. Pearson, had recommended that Taylor enroll at BC's night school to take some classes to boost his GPA. If he took three classes during each of the summer sessions and earned A's, he could bring his transferable GPA up above 3.0 and be back to where he used to stand academically. This gave Taylor some hope that, even if he couldn't play football, he could finish his business degree at a distinguished institution. It was going to be rather humbling to attend night school where his younger brother Marc would be a full-time student. However, Taylor knew he could not allow his pride to stand in his way.

Taylor had never expected to run into Michelle Taylor or Katie McKnight while visiting his former college. It seemed like a twist of fate, as if he was meant to know for certain that his brother Jordan had never tried to take advantage of Michelle. However, Taylor had been left wondering if Michelle still had feelings for Marc or if she was only into Jordan. How his two younger brothers had managed to entangle themselves in a love triangle while Jordan was numerous states away was beyond Taylor.

Michelle was beautiful and kind, so Taylor could understand why his brothers cared for her, but to let her come between their relationship was immature. Taylor knew Jordan had tried his best to explain himself and mend things with Marc, but Marc was stubborn—the most stubborn person in their family. He had high standards for himself and for others. If anyone fell below those standards, he typically shut them out of his life. Taylor could not help but wonder if Marc realized resentment was keeping him from discovering the truth about what had actually happened to Michelle.

Taylor pulled his phone out of his pocket and plugged it into his charger before beginning his ride back to Southie. As he was driving, he noticed that his radio, which displayed text alerts and missed calls, said he had a missed call from Marc. Taylor's heart leaped in his chest. He immediately wondered if Marc had called him by accident, but then noticed the screen also showed he had a voicemail. As he hit the button to play the message, he felt a mixture of nerves and curiosity. Had Cathy told Marc she had seen him? Had Marc called to berate him for selling more drugs to Luke?

Upon playing the message, Taylor was stunned to hear that Marc wanted to visit him and relieved that he did not sound angry. It brought Taylor immense comfort to hear his brother's voice, so he immediately called him back. His heart pounded in his chest as he waited for Marc to answer.

"Hello?" Marc's voice rang through Taylor's Bluetooth radio a moment later.

"Hey, I just got your message. Sorry, I was at a meeting at Northeastern when you called," Taylor replied, hoping the news would please his brother.

"Oh," Marc commented, sounding surprised. "Well, I'm in the city, and I wanted to stop by your place if you're around."

"I'm heading home from campus right now," Taylor informed him. "I'll be home all night."

"Where do you even live?" Marc asked.

"In a condo on Broadway in Southie," Taylor replied. "I'll text you the address. What time do you want to come by?"

"Well, I'm heading to dinner now, but I can come over after. We're going to Maggiano's, and a family-style dinner there isn't quick. I could probably get to your place by seven. I can't stay too long because I have tickets for the Bruins game."

"You'll miss first period if you come at seven," Taylor reasoned.

"It's fine. We just got the tickets last minute, anyway."

"Okay, well, I'll see you in a couple hours then," Taylor stated happily.

"Sounds good. I'll call if I have any trouble finding it."

"All right. Later," Taylor said before ending the call. Marc did not sound upset, so Taylor doubted Cathy or Luke had mentioned anything about their visit.

Before Taylor reached his condo, a call came through from his father. He answered, assuming his dad was calling to talk him into coming home for Easter.

"We're going to church at eleven and then eating around two," his father said. "Jordan's flying in tonight, and everyone wants to see you."

"I would say except for Marc, but he's actually coming by my place later," Taylor stated.

"He is?" his father asked, sounding surprised.

"Yup. I don't know why, but he's coming over before the Bruins game."

"He had a meeting at BC today. Maybe he has some good news to share with you."

"I doubt he'd care to share any good news with me," Taylor remarked. "Maybe Chris put him up to it. Chris called earlier and invited me to his house for Easter."

"You should come," his father stated. "We're your family, and we want to support you while you fix things."

Taylor sighed. "I know. I'm just embarrassed."

"Of who you were, not who you are today."

"That's not true; I hate where I am today."

"It's a lot better than where you were when I found you on your bathroom floor."

"True. I met with my advisor at NU today. If I take classes full-time this summer at BC's Woods School, I'll have enough credits to transfer somewhere as a senior."

"That's great, T," his dad said. "When can you enroll?"

"Summer classes start in May, so I should register soon."

"I know you haven't asked, but we'll obviously pay your tuition."

"No," Taylor stated firmly. "You've already given me money for my rent, and I have money in the bank. I can pay for my summer classes. You guys can pay if I actually get into a college without a scholarship."

"You belong back on the field," his father said. "I'm praying you get that opportunity."

"Me too," Taylor stated. "At least Jordan is being productive. When I was his captain, I honestly questioned if he cared enough about the game to succeed at it. He's matured a lot since high school."

"Yup, Jordan pulled it together," his father said. "I can't say we're not proud, but you're the one with the gift."

"Yeah, well, a gift doesn't get you anywhere if you let yourself get side-tracked."

"Very true," his father remarked. "We're picking Jordan up at the airport tonight. He'd like it if you came home for Easter. He's coming home to see you."

"Me and the girl he likes," Taylor commented.

"Oh, did you talk to him?"

"No, I ran into her at Northeastern. She was on a college tour—Marc's friend, Michelle."

Mr. Dunkin laughed. "Leave it to your brother to have the pick of the litter at Notre Dame but still need to one-up Marc. I know Michelle. Marc's loved her since he hit puberty."

"Well, thankfully that's a mess I have nothing to do with. I'll consider coming home Sunday based on how things go with Marc tonight."

"I'm surprised he called you," his father admitted. "I've been telling him to for months, but he's so darn stubborn. He'll forgive you in due time. He just has a hard time letting go of the past."

"I think I do too," Taylor said.

"**You** need to forgive yourself for what happened last year," his father admonished him. "Maybe once you forgive yourself and spend some time with our family, Marc will follow your lead."

Taylor knew his father was speaking with wisdom; he did need to forgive himself. That would have been a lot easier with Marc's support. He loathed himself for ruining their relationship.

"Marc told me about some of the things Chris got into last year. I'm sure there's more to it than what he told us, but Chris is doing great now. Your uncle Mike and aunt Jen are responsible for his issues. Don't carry that on your shoulders. Your aunt and uncle need to get their priorities straight. Their daughter has slipped up and called your mother 'Mom' on a few occasions. We have no problem babysitting Katie, but she's twelve years old, and she needs her parents. Chris is lucky to have grown up with you, Jordan, and Marc like brothers."

"I'm proud of Chris," Taylor stated. "He's a lot smarter than I ever thought."

"He tapped into the greatest power on Earth. It's the strength that has kept me on the straight-and-narrow for over fifteen years. Let it get a grip on you, and you'll see doors open that no man could ever shut."

Chapter 2

Fifteen minutes later, Cathy Kagelli was sitting between Luke Davids and Marc Dunkin at a booth inside Maggiano's. As excited as she was for a cheese-filled Italian feast, she was nervous to spend time around Michelle. As Marc's only ex-girlfriend, Michelle was still on his pedestal. Moreover, she was the most beautiful girl at Montgomery Lake High. Cathy felt small in comparison.

According to Marc, Michelle was his best friend—someone he looked out for and loved like family. He claimed to no longer have romantic feelings for her, but Cathy could not understand how that was possible. Michelle was the closest thing to "perfect" Cathy had ever seen. She was warm, engaging, smart, and level-head; she was a virgin with rock-solid Christian morals and an interest in helping others; and on top of that, she was humble.

As soon as Michelle entered the restaurant's dining room, Cathy locked her eyes on Michelle's long chestnut-brown hair. Michelle's friend Katie was also very pretty with long dirty-blonde hair and a stunning smile. Katie had been dating Matt Davids when Cathy had first met Jason. Now Katie was dating Andy Rosetti's older brother, Robby.

"Marc, you will not believe who we ran into today!" Michelle exclaimed as soon as she reached the table. "Hi Luke! Hi Cathy."

"Shells! Katie!" Luke exclaimed and stood up to hug them.

"Hi," Cathy responded shyly.

Marc laughed. "Who did you see?"

"Taylor!" Michelle replied. "At Northeastern. He looked great!"

Marc's facial expression grew a bit tense at the sound of Taylor's name. Cathy found it rather ironic that everyone at the table, aside from Marc, had seen his brother that day. She was dreading the ride to South Boston before the Bruins game. Knowing herself all too well, she feared her conscience would get the best of her and that she would tell Marc she had seen Taylor. As much as she hated keeping it from him, she was afraid that telling him would keep him from visiting Taylor. After realizing that Taylor was sober and considering going back to college, she wanted Marc to make amends with him. She knew, first hand, what it was like to have a drug takeover your personality and how important it was to have people to rely on while trying to get sober. Although she did not know for certain, she believed Marc and Taylor's falling out had been over Luke. After her discussion with Luke during lunch, she had realized there was a decent chance Marc knew more about her and Luke's drug history than what she had presumed.

Other Books by Stacy A. Padula

Gripped Part 1: The Truth We Never Told

In high school, Taylor Dunkin broke more records than any other athlete to step foot in Montgomery, Massachusetts. As a sophomore in college, he was ranked by ESPN as one of the NFL's top 100 prospects. However, his aspirations came to a jarring halt when a knee injury and two surgeries left him sidelined.

One year later, Taylor is a person of interest in a highly confidential investigation headed by the Boston Police Department. He has entangled himself in a crime ring notorious for pushing opiates, cocaine, and benzodiazepines on local college campuses. When Taylor's younger brother Marc discovers that Taylor is behind the copious drug supply circulating around Montgomery Lake High School, he sets off to not only reverse the damage Taylor has caused, but also save his lifelong role model from becoming a casualty of America's deadly opioid epidemic.

Montgomery Lake High #1: The Right Person

Growing up in the shadow of two NFL-destined cousins, Chris Dunkin has high hopes for his own future in football. However, a drug addiction threatens to destroy everything he has worked hard to attain. When Chris meets Courtney Angeletti—the mayor's straightedge Christian daughter—he believes she could be the source of inspiration he needs to overcome his destructive lifestyle. Courtney, however, has other ideas.

The desire to rebel has been tugging on Courtney's heartstrings for some time, and Chris's "bad-boy" reputation draws her to him like a moth to a flame. After all, he is a central part of the most popular clique in her high school. Will Chris pull Courtney away from her faith or will Courtney inspire him to overcome his rebellious lifestyle?

Montgomery Lake High #2: When Darkness Tries to Hide

A powerful supercell is spawning above Montgomery Lake High School, while a separate storm is brewing in its halls. The question is which one should Cathy Kagelli, Jason Davids, and their friends fear the most?

Montgomery Lake High #3: The Aftermath

At age fifteen, Jason Davids appears to have it all: high grades, popular friends, a beautiful girlfriend, and nearly any worldly thing that promises enjoyment at his disposal. Despite this, there is a persistent emptiness inside his heart. After failing to fill the void with achievements, relationships, and illicit substances, Jason finds himself intrigued by Jessie: a rather quiet girl, who is the daughter of a local pastor. How is it possible that she stands for everything his lifestyle opposes yet possesses the one thing he has been searching for all along?

Montgomery Lake High #4: The Battle for Innocence

Jon Anderson and Chantal Kagelli are trying to live moral lives, but temptations are plaguing them in and out of school. Will they continue to be lights in their best friends' lives or will they get pulled into the darkness?

Montgomery Lake High #5: The Forces Within

After being trapped inside his own body, unable to communicate with anyone but his own thoughts, Andy Rosetti finally wakes up from the coma that controlled his life for one month. But upon awakening, Andy finds himself and his friends in an unfamiliar setting: a mansion riddled with secret passages and supernatural forces. As his friends fall prey to the entities surrounding them, Andy must figure out if the darkness lies within the mansion's walls or within the people surrounding him.

About the Author

Stacy A. Padula, a native of Pembroke, Massachusetts, has accrued years of experience working with adolescents. She has been a mentor, life coach, youth group leader, and private educational consultant with extensive experience in the fields of college counseling, tutoring, and standardized test preparation. She is the Founder and President of South Shore College Consulting & Tutoring based in Plymouth, Massachusetts.

Awards: Stacy was in Marquis Who's Who in America (2018) for excellence in literature and education. She was also featured in Cambridge Who's Who for Young Professionals (2009) and Marquis Who's Who in the World (2018 & 2019). In 2018, she was also awarded the Albert Nelson Lifetime Achievement award, and in 2019, the International Association of Top Professionals chose Stacy Padula as their "Top Educational Consultant of the Year."

Publications: Stacy's first novel, "The Right Person," was published in 2010. In 2011, "When Darkness Tries to Hide" was published, followed by "The Aftermath" (Padula's personal favorite) in 2013. In 2014, both "The Battle for Innocence" and "The Forces Within" were released, and in 2015, all five books hit the shelves of Barnes & Noble. For Stacy, it was a dream come true to see her books for sale in the popular, mainstream bookstore! In 2016, Barnes & Noble chose Stacy to be a featured author for its teen book festival. In 2019, she released a new book series called "Gripped," which chronicles how good kids become drug addicts.

Background: Stacy was a Presidential Scholar and on the Dean's List at Wentworth, where she studied Architecture and Interior Design. After graduation, she worked at an architecture firm in Boston for two years. Although she enjoyed her work, she felt something was missing—she wanted to spend more time helping people grow academically and spiritually. For close to a year, she split her time between tutoring, writing, and working at a design firm in Plymouth.

When she fell in love with tutoring, she left the A&D industry completely and took a full-time position with an educational company. She attained tutoring certification in 2009 through The International Tutor Association. Her career took off, and within one year, she was promoted to Program Director. Stacy knew she had found her niche! During her eight years with that company, she received multiple promotions and held a variety of titles, including Manager of Curriculum & Instruction and Director of Operations. In 2016, Stacy founded South Shore College Consulting & Tutoring.

Stacy writes young adult novels in the hopes of preparing teens to face the "war zone" that is high school—to help kids deal with the stress and peer pressure and to encourage them to "steer a straight path, pursue God, and not fall for the false promises of the world."

In her spare time, Stacy enjoys skiing, going to Bruins games, reading about psychology, taking her dogs to the beach, and spending time with her family, husband Tim, and friends.

Connect With Us!

Stacy's Instagram @author_stacypadula
Stacy's Twitter @MLHBookSeries
Cathy's Instagram @ckagelli99
Chantal's Instagram @chantal_kagelli
Jason's Instagram @jds_on
Lisa's Instagram @lisa_ankerman99
Chris's Instagram @dunkin_85
Luke's Instagram @lukedavids97
Alyssa's Instagram @alyssa_kelly02
Website www.stacyapadula.com

Did You Enjoy Gripped Part 2?

If you loved this book, would you please leave a review on Amazon?

CPSIA information can be obtained
at www.ICGtesting.com
Printed in the USA
BVHW032136010819
554943BV00001B/59/P

9 781733 153607